The Year of Sunshine

Monica Geti

NEW HOLLAND

First published in Australia in 2004 by
New Holland Publishers (Australia) Pty Ltd
Sydney • Auckland • London • Cape Town

14 Aquatic Drive Frenchs Forest NSW 2086 Australia
218 Lake Road Northcote Auckland New Zealand
86 Edgware Road London W2 2EA United Kingdom
80 McKenzie Street Cape Town 8001 South Africa

Copyright © 2004 in text: Monica Geti
Copyright © 2004 New Holland Publishers (Australia) Pty Ltd

All rights reserved. No part of this publication may be reproduced, stored in a retrieval system or transmitted, in any form or by any means, electronic, mechanical, photocopying, recording or otherwise, without the prior written permission of the publishers and copyright holders.

2 4 6 8 10 9 7 5 3 1

National Library of Australia Cataloguing-in-Publication Data:

Geti, Monica, 1939—.
The year of sunshine.

ISBN 1 74110 181 6.

1. Geti, Monica, 1939-.—Journeys—Mediterranean Sea.
2. Geti, Monica, 1939-.—Marriage. 3. Voyages and travels.
4. Mediterranean Sea—Description and travel. I. Title.

910.91822

Managing Editor: Monica Berton
Copy Editor: Jenny Hunter
Designer: Karl Roper
Printer: Griffin Press, Adelaide
Cover image: Getty Images

This book was typeset in Bergamo 11 pt

Contents

Acknowledgements 5

Chapter 1:
The Decision 7

Chapter 2:
A Journey of a Thousand Miles
Begins with a Single Step 25

Chapter 3:
Destiny Unknown 43

Chapter 4:
Searching the Italian Riviera 53

Chapter 5:
Searching France and Spain 65

Chapter 6:
Sunshine is Born 77

Chapter 7:
A Temporary Truce is Declared 103

Chapter 8:
Antibes 131

Chapter 9:
Port Grimaud 151

Chapter 10:
Decisions, Decisions 169

Chapter 11:
Breakthrough 179

Chapter 12:
Success 187

Epilogue 205

About the Author 208

To my darling husband
For always being there for me
And without whom this book could never have existed

To my darling daughters
For always being there for me

To Sunshine
For just being there

Acknowledgements

A big thank you to my family for their love and support through the ups and downs of both the living through and the writing of *The Year of Sunshine*.

Another big thank you to all the people we met through that year and who helped us make the journey so memorable.

In some cases, places and names and incidental details have been changed to protect privacy and any similarity is purely coincidental.

The author and publisher are grateful for permission to reproduce copyright material from *Footprints on the Path*, copyright Eileen Caddy 1976, published by Findhorn Press, Scotland.

Chapter 1

The Decision

He wanted us to retire on a sailboat. I did not. We fought. He won. It was as simple as that—or should have been.

In fact, it was not. But I could not know that at the start. My imagination was already running wild as I armed myself with jars of mini-facials, endless books for him and me, a chess set and a year's supply of vitamins, but nothing could have prepared me for what lay ahead as I reluctantly set off for uncharted waters.

A crowd of family and friends came to the airport to see us off. We said our goodbyes—hugs, kisses and tears all round.

'Take care of your grandmother.'

'Yes. Don't worry about a thing.'

'Call us if you need anything.'

'Don't do anything crazy, Francesca, and look after your sister. Natasha, please keep an eye on Francesca and Nonna.'

'Yes, don't worry. Don't you two do anything crazy.'

'Bye, I love you.'

The Year of Sunshine

After a final round of kisses, Marco picked up the bags and we started walking towards passport control. I looked back and ran over and kissed them all again. As we went through the door, I wiped the tears from my face. I was wearing the T-shirt the girls had given me with a photo of them both screen-printed on the front, and hugged it closer to me. Marco was happy we were going, but moody because he knew I was not one hundred per cent with him. We found our seats on the plane and sat holding hands.

He leaned over and kissed me. 'I love you,' he said and I knew he meant thank you for coming, thank you for doing this for me. 'You're going to love sailing the Mediterranean, you'll see. Life in the marinas is a lot of fun.' And then he turned his attention to his yachting magazines. Oh God, I hope so, I thought as I stared out the window, not seeing a thing.

If ever there was a time in my life when I felt I was jumping into a void, this was it. We had jumped into the unknown many times before and landed on our feet. Or if we hadn't, we'd scrambled up and recovered; but we were younger then and we'd done it without thinking, and our only goal was to have an adventure. This was different. We were older and we'd done a lot of thinking and discussing. And, crucially, we weren't united on this one. We had different values now and different needs; and I wondered whether I would ever come to see his point of view or if he would ever see mine. Thank God we still loved each other, that should help.

I knew this was make or break time for our relationship. Scary enough if I had been on home turf, but scarier still in

The Decision

unfamiliar territory without the support of family or friends. I was on my own and felt desolate.

Someone once told me to enjoy the eternal now, but what was there to enjoy about this? Oh yes, the jump into the unknown. At least I was holding hands with someone who loved me; but how much longer would he love me if I was unable to enjoy his dream with him. I felt it was up to me to help him through this crisis, but who was going to help me?

I closed my eyes and prayed for the relief of drifting off, to escape my ever-present doubts.

It was many months later, that Marco told me of the desperation he felt on the morning of his decision. Had he told me earlier, things might have been different. He recounted his story in detail.

As usual, he had gone out on to our balcony overlooking the ocean to drink his coffee while waiting for me to get ready to leave for the office.

'It lay before me as if tempting me,' he began. 'That day it was calm, the sky was an intense blue and there wasn't a breath of wind.

'I took my coffee over to the railing and leant on it and stared at the ocean but after a few minutes I didn't really see it. I was in very low spirits and could see no future for myself. My thoughts played over and over, as if someone had pressed a repeat button in my brain.

'I was 51 years old. What was I doing with my life? It was seven o'clock in the morning, and here I was, doing the same thing I'd done morning after morning—drinking my coffee, waiting for you, going to the office, sitting in front of a computer all day, coming home, having dinner, going to bed, then waking up and doing it all over again, and again.

'I'd been thinking about my life a lot lately, questioning everything—past, present and future. I thought about our daughters, our beautiful daughters. They're such great kids and I'm so proud of them. But they were grown-up, and I was a much smaller part of their lives now. You'd recently given up your career and joined me in my business, just for something to do.

'I thought about my career. I was a partner in a successful company. We lived in Sydney, one of the most beautiful cities in the world. But something was missing—this wasn't enough. It was becoming an obsession, a riddle, going round and round. I'd been trying to find some answers, but my thoughts only went in circles. And I kept coming back to the same question—what do I want out of life now? I'd done what I had set out to do. I felt I'd provided you and the girls with everything you needed—love, home, travel and a good education. But now *I* needed something—I felt empty.

'While I was standing there, a group of young surfers made their way down the cliffs to the water. They were laughing, noisy and excited, and made me think of my own youth.

'When I was young it was so easy to dream of the future, but now I was in that future and I couldn't see what was ahead for me. It was very depressing.

'All my life I've loved travelling, revelling in discovering new places, new ways of life, new foods. Like a true Italian, good food has always been important to me, comparable to good sex.

The Decision

'I often think back to eating a *feijoada* in Brazil, a delicious *parrillada* with *guasacaca* in Argentina, or an *arepa* with *mondongo* in Venezuela. Or, in my mind, I might fly north, stopping in Maine for a clam chowder and a lobster tail. Further north still, I stop in Canada for a ham steak with pineapple and mashed potatoes. Or, I might cross the Atlantic to England, and have some fish and chips or hot salted beef. Then, perhaps, across the Channel to France for a bouillabaisse.

'I could spend a day just dreaming about the food of Tuscany. And it isn't just the food, but the customs, the idiosyncracies, the varieties, the people. God, I missed it.

'You know I adore you and the girls, and for your sake and stability, I was happy to make Sydney our base for the last 20 years. But the reasons for doing this didn't exist any more. I could have gone on making money—but why? So I could leave more for the kids when I die, for them to travel first class. How much money is enough and, anyway, life had to be about more than money.

'I felt that the months of thinking about this were going to make my brain explode. Finally, that morning, I knew I had to decide what I wanted to do for the rest of my life. But what could I do?

'Ideally, I wanted to start travelling again, as we used to before we settled in Sydney. That would have meant retiring to do it properly—to be really free. That appealed. But not the thought of travelling from hotel room to hotel room—that didn't fit into what I was seeking.

'We'd lived in some of the world's great places including London, Paris, Rome, South and North America. So the

The Year of Sunshine

idea of moving from Sydney to another beautiful city didn't appeal. I realised that if I was going to travel again, I wanted to approach it differently.'

He'd continued thinking this way, he told me, and then the ocean came back into focus, the waves rippling gently in the sun.

'And then a thought struck me,' he said. 'How about from the water? I could approach life from the water.

'I thought about that for a bit and then looked down. My cup was empty. I had drunk it without realising. Is that how I was now living my life? The thought frightened me, and made me more determined to make a decision that morning.

'I didn't want my dream of travelling again to be postponed, and so I decided, then and there, that's what I was going to do—I was going to approach life from the water.'

He said he'd come inside and felt more optimistic than he had for a long time. And I recall seeing him smiling again, unusual during this period because he'd been grumpy and stressed.

He had asked me to book a cabin on a cruise. I'd assumed it was to cheer him up and I thought it was a good idea. I managed to get a cancelled cabin on a cruise to Fiji, Pago Pago, Bora Bora, Moorea and Tahiti, leaving in two weeks' time.

It was during the cruise, while sunbathing and drinking fruit-punch cocktails, that he said, 'You know, I've been thinking,' and then he outlined his plan for us to retire to a sailboat on the Mediterranean.

'I've had enough of the business world and its unrelenting commitments. I want to travel again. I want to be free again. I'm going to retire and buy a comfortable sailboat with two

The Decision

bedrooms, two bathrooms and all the possible comforts. We'll be able to get to places we haven't seen yet like Sardinia, Majorca, and Greece.

'If I was a multi-millionaire, I'd buy a 50-metre yacht with captain and crew, but I'm not, so I'll have to think in terms of 12–14 metres, I'll be the captain and you'll be the crew. That's what I am going to do. What do you think?'

'I think it stinks!'

Unfortunately, it hadn't occurred to him that I might not like the idea.

I was furious.

'Why would you make a decision like that without consulting me first? I don't want to retire. You know how I hated it when I sold the boutique. I was like a fish out of water for months until you asked me to help out in the office, and now that I am back in the business world you want to take it away from me. And sailing? Why sailing? We don't know how to sail.'

'That's what makes it exciting, we've never done it before.'

'Well, it doesn't appeal to me at all. Not one tiny bit.'

I was seething with anger and hurt. The business I'd built up over 12 years had come to an untimely end when the combination of a spiralling exchange rate and a rent increase made it untenable. I'd grieved for it, almost like a death in the family. After it was gone, I renovated the apartment, then found myself deadly bored. Since then I'd been trying to find something to fulfil me. I needed to be busy, to feel the satisfaction of achievement, and I certainly could not see that happening while lazing about on a sailboat with nothing to do but sunbathe all day, maybe all year.

The Year of Sunshine

'How could sailing on the Mediterranean not appeal to you?' he asked angrily. 'It would appeal to anyone but you. Why must you relate your sense of achievement and satisfaction to working? Can't you get satisfaction from just living and having fun? You used to be able to. Why is it necessary for you to work to achieve satisfaction?'

'Well, that's only part of it,' I said. 'I don't like that you decided for me. I don't want to be retired, and I certainly don't want to live on a boat. You know I can't stand the damp. We don't know how to sail, you're not in the least bit handy and you have no idea how to fix anything—I end up fixing everything.'

'Well, I don't see any of that as a problem.'

How typically male, I thought.

'But I won't like it,' I said, determined.

'How do you know, you've never done it.'

'I just know, and I'll be bored.'

'How could you be bored travelling to different places all the time? I just can't see it. Why are you being so unreasonable?'

'I'm afraid of the ocean!'

'But we live right over the ocean for God's sake, and you love it there.'

Yes, and I saw how unpredictable it was, changing from sparkling blue to blustery grey in minutes, and I took comfort from being in my living room, safe from the elements.

'I won't like living on a boat, I tell you.'

'Are you afraid on this boat?'

'Of course not, but this is a luxury liner with a captain and crew if anything goes wrong. That's quite different. What a ridiculous thing to ask.'

The Decision

'No, it's not. You're on a boat on the water. It's the same thing.'

'I really don't want to do this, Marco.'

'Well, I really do.'

We hardly noticed the rest of our holiday. The exotic ports came and went. We went through the motions, took photos, but we were both preoccupied with what was going to happen to our future.

One of the things that bothered me about Marco's plan was the fact that since I'd given up my business, I finally had time to nurture my relationship with my daughters. I had missed much of their growing up, and now I had the time to make it up to them. While working I'd tried to give them quality because I certainly hadn't been able to give them quantity. I'd worked six days a week and gone to Europe twice a year on buying trips. They had grown up with a working mother, and had been looked after by their Nonna, who was vigilant in her care of them. But now we enjoyed a close relationship and I didn't want to leave them again. I needed them and they needed me. When I pointed this out to Marco during one of our many heated discussions, his reply was predictable.

'But they're grown up, for Christ's sake. Francesca's 20 next year and Natasha's 26. They don't need us around telling them what to do. They were fine when you were overseas and they were only teenagers then. You may need them, but they don't need you.'

'But what about your mother?'

'My mother is fine. Francesca takes good care of her. They take care of each other.'

The Year of Sunshine

It was true—Francesca and her Italian grandmother had a great relationship. Natasha had moved into her own place so she was not around so much. Nonna had been ever-present in the girls' lives in my absences. She had lived with us for many years and I loved her a lot. She was a surrogate mother to me and my girls—always there for us. She was getting on in years and I knew she would miss us. I felt guilty and angry. Guilty at him for considering leaving our daughters and his mother, and angry that he had decided that I should leave them too. I didn't want to leave them, how could he?

'I'm going to do this, Angel, so you'd better get used to the idea. I need to do it.'

'But why must you retire so young? You've still got ten good years ahead of you.'

'I don't want to work for the next ten years. I want my life back, and I want you back.'

'Well, you're not going to get me in this frame of mind, are you? And what's wrong with me?'

'You've changed. Your values are different.'

'Of course they're different, we all change.'

'Yes, but your values are wrong now.'

'And who appointed you God?'

It was a bitter battle.

Marco and I had been through a lot together. We met in London 30 years ago, fell deliriously in love, and left London together two weeks later. He was Italian and had spent the last few years in South America. I was born and bred English. After we left England, we travelled and worked in different countries, in different languages, and

The Decision

had many adventures until we arrived in Australia where we decided to settle down for our two young children. I loved him very much and would do almost anything for him, and he knew it, but I considered this overstepping the mark.

Besides, I was rebuilding my life without my beloved boutique. I loved Sydney and my apartment on the cliffs overlooking the ocean. It was one of my regrets that I'd never had time to appreciate my adopted home while I was busy working. Now, I finally had the time to appreciate its golden coastline, the magnificent harbour and opera house, the beautiful parks, and world-class restaurants and cafés. I almost envied girlfriends and clients who told me of leisurely al fresco lunches, in the sun, at promenade restaurants. I had rarely seen the outside of my boutique except when I left it to go on buying trips, and I had intended to change that. I had intended to find part-time work, fashion consulting or something similar, to fulfil my ambition, but still leave me time to enjoy friends and family, and get to know Sydney. I felt that at 50, I was too young and active to retire.

I certainly didn't need to be taken away and planted on a sailboat in the middle of the ocean away from everybody and everything. It sounded like purgatory.

I thought I'd try reasoning with him. It worked sometimes.

'Marco, what about a long holiday? Say we take a year off. Wouldn't that be great?' I was prepared to put my plans on hold for a short while, but not forever.

'No, I don't want to go away worrying about anything. I need to be free. I'm going to retire. I'm going to do this with or without you, but I'd rather do it with you. Think about that.'

The Year of Sunshine

The resolution in his voice and his choice of words—'with or without you' and 'think about that'—told me there was little chance of his backing down. I was stunned that he was prepared to sacrifice our marriage if I wasn't prepared to go along with his plan.

He had been a wonderful husband and father, and we had had so many great times together. He had always loved me passionately and devotedly, and I loved him deeply. What was this huge chasm that had appeared in our lives? We suddenly had different needs, opposite needs, and felt equally determined about them.

'Can't you understand that my spirit is dying?' he asked, his tone impassioned.

'Can't you understand that my spirit will die if you take me away from here?' I shot back.

We were well and truly locked in battle.

I discussed Marco's decision endlessly with my daughters and friends. Francesca and Natasha were shocked.

'Do you think he'll really do it?' they asked.

I nodded.

'I can't really see you in that kind of life. You don't even like swimming,' added Francesca.

'Oh my God, what am I going to do?' I implored.

'You know it might not be so bad.' This was Francesca speaking again. She was thinking of holidays in the South of France on a yacht. At 20, she couldn't see the complexity of it.

'You might have to go, Mummy, you know when Daddy's got his mind set on something nothing can change it.' This was Natasha's contribution.

The Decision

'But I don't want to leave you both.'

'Don't worry, we'll come and visit.'

I could see that, in a way, they were proud of their father's courage to give up success for what he believed in. But where did that leave me?

'We'll write to you all the time.'

'You won't even know where I am.' Angry tears filled my eyes.

Friends convinced me I was right. 'You sailing. It's not for you.'

'I know, but he's adamant.'

'Don't go!'

'But then I'd lose him.'

'Oh, he'll be back.'

'I wouldn't count on it—he seems to be having a mid-life crisis.'

Someone suggested we should take sailing lessons first to see if we liked it. I was less than enthusiastic.

'You've lost your spirit of adventure,' Marco accused me. 'You've got set in your ways, that's the problem.'

It was intended to provoke and hit its target.

We signed up for a special deal—four lessons with a free one thrown in. We took them over the Christmas–New Year period which is usually hot but, just to add to my discomfort, that year was stormy, rainy and cold. I'd had enough after the first two lessons to know that I passionately disliked it. The small sailing dinghy on which we were learning was tossed about on a black and moody ocean with a matching sky above. Cold spray stung my cheeks and the wind whipped my hair. I was cold, wet and scared. I felt totally insecure in that toy boat, and one glance at the crumpled T-shirts and shorts, and wind-burnt faces was enough to convince me that this was definitely not for me. I let them keep their free lesson.

He didn't enjoy it either.

'But on the Mediterranean it will be different,' he assured me. 'We'll have a much bigger boat, plus we'll have in-mast sails and an electric anchor.'

I knew he wouldn't like the physical aspect. He was a keen bridge player and could sit for hours. Hoisting the sail would definitely not be in his vocabulary. I had hoped that would be the last I heard of the sailboat, but he began organising our business affairs and preparing legal papers relating to the sale of his share of the company. Towards the end of December, he was free.

Still our battle raged.

He obviously was going to do it, with or without me. But he seemed to be including me in his preparations at this point, even against my will. However, a last minute change in plans never fazed Marco.

'I will take a long holiday with you, but retirement, no.'

'No holiday, I am retiring for good.'

'Then go on your own.'

'Think about that ...'

We'll just take a holiday and be back, I kept telling myself, with memories flooding my mind of other trips, some cut short by work pressures and others interrupted by phone calls to Australia every second day.

Nobody had thought he would go through with it, considering him too young to retire, but the wanderlust of our

The Decision

earlier years together had recaptured him. He was ecstatically happy and was looking forward to his boat and his exciting, adventurous new life. He could talk of nothing else.

I, on the other hand, was very unhappy, and had still not made up my mind whether I would go or not.

When the anger occasionally subsided, he tried coaxing me with things he knew I would like.

'We could stop over in Hong Kong, you enjoyed that last time.'

I admitted I would enjoy that.

'You've always dreamed about owning a Jaguar. What about if we buy a second-hand one in England, and drive to the Continent. We could spend a few weeks in the Alps.'

It was all very tempting, but was I prepared to be bought and at what price? He took it for granted I would follow him as blindly as I had so many times before. But I'd changed over the last 20 years. I felt that if I agreed to go I was doing so because I no longer had control over my life and I resented being asked to give that up. If I went I'd be doing it because I loved him, but I wanted to make the choice. I wouldn't go because my needs were less important than his. Surely love cannot demand such sacrifices. Until this point, I believed we had a good understanding of each other but now I was beginning to have my doubts. Then again, I couldn't imagine my life without Marco. Nor did I want to.

'Do I dig my heels in and spend the rest of my life alone, or do I give in and lose respect for myself?' I pondered incessantly.

The Year of Sunshine

Emotions, questions, solutions, imagined outcomes and compromises filled my head day and night. Many times, I cried myself silently to sleep.

Time was passing. He was planning to leave around mid-February.

For Christmas I received three copies of Kay Cottee's *First Lady* from friends who were half-amused, half-concerned for me and curious about the outcome of our battle. It was the story of an Australian woman who became the first in history to complete a solo non-stop and unassisted voyage around the globe. I finished the book quickly, eager to see how she managed, then threw it across the room in anger, more convinced I would never be able to cope.

Marco was busy tying up the loose ends of the business deal and preparing lists of things to do, buy and take.

My heart was growing smaller and smaller, painfully aware of where this activity was leading. Decisions had to be made. Were my values wrong now? Was I being self-focused? Self-doubt was creeping in. We had our differences, but we still loved each other. If he's this determined, I thought, maybe his spirit is dying because he was, apparently, prepared to give up everything we had achieved during our 30 years together. How could he give that up so easily? I felt I didn't know him any more. I could already see the change in him just from the preparation for his new life. He was alive again, full of ideas and fiercely determined.

I didn't want to lose him. He infuriated me but he excited me. It was his indomitable passion for life and his insatiable appetite for adventure that had made me fall in

The Decision

love with him so many years ago and, so, although still reluctant, I made my decision.

What the hell, I could always come home!

Chapter 2

A Journey of a Thousand Miles Begins with a Single Step

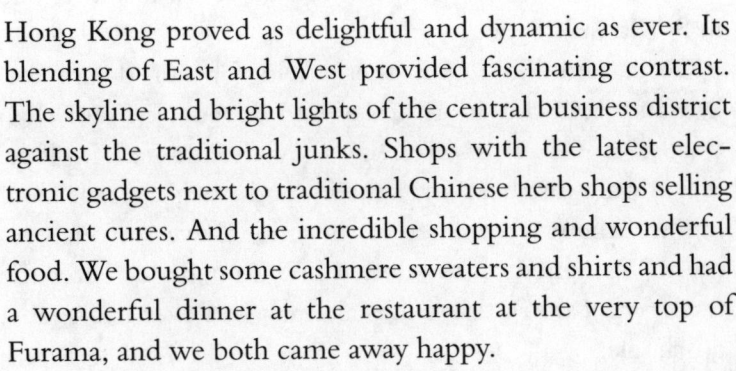

Hong Kong proved as delightful and dynamic as ever. Its blending of East and West provided fascinating contrast. The skyline and bright lights of the central business district against the traditional junks. Shops with the latest electronic gadgets next to traditional Chinese herb shops selling ancient cures. And the incredible shopping and wonderful food. We bought some cashmere sweaters and shirts and had a wonderful dinner at the restaurant at the very top of Furama, and we both came away happy.

The Year of Sunshine

London was busy as we searched for the car in typical Marco style—rushing everywhere and not missing a single car dealer. We wanted a second-hand Jaguar. We would get the paper early and start phoning, making appointments back-to-back all day, and dash from one to the other. We would arrive breathless with anticipation, only to be disappointed. The colour was wrong, the model was wrong, or the price was wrong.

It looked as though this was going to take a little longer than we thought so we decided to move into a studio in central London. We even asked the studio owner to help us look for the car and he put us in touch with a friend of his, but it wasn't the right car.

Most nights we would arrive at Harrods just before it closed, and would choose what we'd cook for dinner from the varied and exotic array in the Food Hall.

We took the opportunity to see some shows. We love theatre in London and on previous trips, if we had a two-day stopover and could fit it in, we would be extravagant and see two shows in one day—the matinee and the evening performance. And in between, we'd eat at our favourite pub in St Martin's Lane.

We started looking further afield for our dream car. We answered ads in Bromley and Sevenoaks, and then finally, at Gerrards Cross, we saw it and fell in love. It had only just been brought in, and wasn't yet cleaned, but we knew we wanted it the minute we set our eyes on it. We signed on the dotted line immediately after the test drive. I don't think the salesman had ever had such a quick sale.

A Journey of a Thousand Miles Begins with a Single Step

Happy and excited with our purchase, we quickly organised the necessary papers, and the very next day we set off for St Moritz. Another inducement for me, before we started on His Big Adventure.

In the past, we had relied on the *Guide Michelin* to help choose our stops. And over the years we'd favoured chateaux, or inns with a bit of character, combining out-of-the-ordinary accommodation with fine French cuisine. They were great in September when the weather was warm, but could be cold and uncomfortable in February with inadequate heating and hot water. But we'd always enjoyed their atmosphere and the superb meals, so decided to try a chateau which featured 'all mod cons'.

We left London around nine in the morning, and made the Dover ferry in time for lunch. Our plan was to arrive at the chateau by four in the afternoon. But as we were ahead of schedule, we decided to continue to another *Guide Michelin* recommendation which we should have reached by about six in the evening.

The car was going beautifully, although we were having some trouble adjusting the heating and air conditioning system. Whenever Marco wanted to know how to do something, I would madly skim through the three-inch thick Jaguar instruction book, while simultaneously reading the map and directing him. Our Jaguar had a computer built into the dashboard and this computer would tell us if anything was wrong. It's a clever thing when you know the meaning of the indicators, but it was new to us. It kept giving us all sorts of messages, which we felt obliged to check, and Marco ended up talking to it like to a troublesome companion.

The Year of Sunshine

'What do you want now?' he would ask.

I didn't realise what was going on until I saw him glaring at the computer screen, trying to decipher the problem. He would then instruct me to quickly find the section on that problem, and tell him what to do.

This didn't prove to be easy, especially when my feet were freezing and burning alternately because I couldn't understand the instructions for the heating system. It wasn't really complicated—my brain was just overloaded.

We had great difficulty finding our chateau in the small French village that had no street lamps. In the end we couldn't find it, so we backtracked and stayed at a small motel near the *sortie* of the *autoroute*.

The next day we reached Switzerland and stayed at Geneva, and pushed on the following morning intending to stop somewhere early afternoon when something appealing turned up. But nothing turned up for hours. We drove on and on into the mountains, snow surrounding us now. Marco was convinced we would find something at Davos. We arrived at Davos at four-thirty and I was expecting to go straight to a hotel, have a hot shower, rest, drinks at an Alpine bar and candlelit dinner—all the things that sound so wonderful when you read about them in a travel book.

Perhaps we could rekindle a little romance. There was still a distance between us and it saddened me. I loved the feel of his arms around me, it made me feel warm and safe, and it hadn't been happening much lately. Here was a chance to get a fresh start in romantic surroundings. But it wasn't to prove so.

A Journey of a Thousand Miles Begins with a Single Step

The hotels uniformly answered, 'Sorry, full.' 'Sorry, booked out.' 'You won't find anything, Davos is full.'

We tried the tourist office but it had closed at five o'clock, five minutes earlier.

'Don't worry,' said Marco. 'St Moritz is only about an hour from here, let's push on.'

I don't think he had bargained on the narrow roads, and our big, wide car. Suffice to say, we arrived in Silva Plana, at the foot of the Julier Pass road, and ten kilometres from St Moritz at about six-thirty. It was one of the few places that had good snow that year, and it was freezing.

We had stayed in Silva Plana the year before and the owner of the ski lodge had been very accommodating in finding us rooms by shuffling some of her bookings around.

'We are sure to find something in the lodge we stayed at last year,' Marco, the optimist, assured me.

'OK, you go up and ask,' I said. I was already tired of this game.

He convinced me to go.

'We're full,' said the owner. 'Silva Plana is full. There's a cross-country skiing marathon on tomorrow, and people from the surrounding villages are here to take part.'

She accompanied me back to the car to greet Marco and report the bad news.

'Don't worry,' Marco told her, 'we'll look around.'

'If you don't find anything,' the hotelier said, 'because I know you and want to help, we have an empty maid's room downstairs which we could offer you, but only if you don't find anything else.'

I shook my head.

The Year of Sunshine

Thank you, but no thank you, I thought.

An hour later, that maid's room was starting to sound like sheer ecstasy.

'I'm afraid it doesn't have a bathroom,' said Frau Pfeiffer, 'you'll have to use the one in the corridor.'

I anticipated being woken several times during the night, if that was the only bathroom.

I had judged correctly, but what I hadn't bargained for was that the bedroom was under the restaurant. Next morning at five, chairs were scraped and tables moved as breakfast was being prepared. I felt I had only just fallen asleep. It didn't matter really; there was no more sleep to be had anyway.

That day, needless to say, we were up bright and early—well, early anyway.

We were early enough to watch the start of the cross-country marathon. It was incredible. Fourteen thousand participants. Fat ones, thin ones, old ones, young ones, all in their skin-tight suits. They just kept coming and coming. It was a sight to see. An army of fluorescent-coloured soldiers brandishing ski stocks, weaving across the lake like a gigantic multi-coloured snake. The sky was a brilliant blue behind them, and the snow shone brightly on the peaks. They skied past the castle at Silva Plana as they made their way to St Moritz. It seemed like a couple of hours later that the last skiers passed and the crowd dispersed.

'If we spend the day looking,' said Marco, 'we are sure to find a room somewhere.'

Marco, financial planner and bridge player, is thorough. We must have searched every type of tourist accommoda-

A Journey of a Thousand Miles
Begins with a Single Step

tion in Silva Plana, St Moritz and neighbouring areas, and we came up with only one possibility other than the maid's room. It was a *hôtel-résidence* (serviced apartment) in St Moritz costing a small Swiss fortune.

I really could not stand the maid's room again, dusk was drawing in and I was starting to get hostile, so Marco persuaded the *résidence* receptionist to let us have the apartment for a week at a reduced price. Marco has many good points, one of which is charm.

St Moritz is so beautiful. It's on the southern side of the Alps in sunny Engadine, and is unique with crystal lakes, forests and majestic glaciers.

I was still having mixed feelings about the trip. My heart was in Sydney with Natasha and Francesca, even though I wanted to re-establish my relationship with Marco. And I can't deny that I was enjoying the car and St Moritz, but I knew what was ahead of me—the dreaded sailboat. Marco was slowly unwinding from the stress that had led up to his retirement decision and the subsequent locking of horns with me, but still had a long way to go.

Watching the cross-country skiing, we realised how out of condition we both were. We started taking walks around the lake and through St Moritz. Its little town centre, delightfully Swiss–German, and the lake is surrounded by elegant hotels. We watched people playing golf on the iced-over lake, and heard there was horse racing on it too.

The second week we were able to find a better-priced studio overlooking the lake. It was magnificent, but we could feel the chill factor coming off the ice and it was a stark contrast to the 30 degrees of the Australian summer I'd left behind. While cold, the weather was still spectacular, and that area one of the most beautiful in the world.

At the end of that week, we decided to move on to Val d'Isere.

We left early. It was a long, tiring trip because we were diverted through the mountains on the way, which added an hour on the journey. We were going via Italy through Aosta and the Col du Petit Saint-Bernard Pass, but when we got there the pass was closed due to ice and snow. At this point, we decided to backtrack to the Tunnel Mont Blanc and make it to Megève for the night.

I love Megève—it held a lot of great memories for us. It's a skiing village in Haute Savoie in the French Alps, and has breathtaking views of Mont Blanc. The town centre is picture-postcard pretty, with its main square surrounded by elegant boutiques and inviting bars and restaurants. Colourfully decorated horse-drawn sleighs wait in line to take you for a ride, and the sound of their hooves and the tinkling of the little bells on the sleigh add to the fairytale atmosphere of the village. In our early days together, when we were working in Geneva, we would ski there at the weekends with a group of friends.

However, this year there was no snow and the slopes were covered, instead, with fresh green grass dotted with yellow buttercups and little alpine flowers in various hues of red, pink, blue and purple.

We decided to stay at Megève a couple of nights to give me a rest from travelling. I have had a back problem since Francesca was born, and the cold and sitting in the car for many hours was aggravating it. However, we agreed to visit

A Journey of a Thousand Miles Begins with a Single Step

Val d'Isere to book a week there, so that we would have a room to go to instead of the tedious job of finding something after hours and hours of driving.

On our way to Val d'Isere, we were both feeling nostalgic for our daughters, perhaps missing their youthful companionship. We passed several hitchhikers whom Marco wanted to pick up. We passed one young man who pointed at our number plates then back to himself, which I interpreted to mean he was English.

Marco said, 'Come on, let's stop.'

'Don't,' I protested, 'it could be dangerous.'

He stopped.

'Thank you so much for picking us up,' said the hitchhiker.

'Us?' I asked.

I looked around and he and another boy were bringing up skis and boxes and brown paper parcels.

'You're totally mad,' I whispered to Marco, in Italian. 'Where do you think you can put the skis?'

'Don't worry,' he replied smiling, 'they can stick out of the car through the window.'

Now I was convinced he was crazy.

The two English boys couldn't believe their luck.

As I turned round to talk to them, I caught a grateful smile from the one we hadn't seen to the one we had stopped for, and I was suddenly glad we had picked them up. I could see they were freezing—they had been waiting nearly two hours, they told us. In fact, the boys kept us amused for a good hour telling us about their hitchhiking travels. I'm sure we became one of those stories.

In the end, we didn't like Val d'Isere, so didn't stay there.

The Year of Sunshine

After three or four days in Megève, we decided to move to Crans Montana in Switzerland. It had been recommended to me by one of my Paris suppliers. Crans and Montana are two separate but neighbouring towns and are generally known as Crans Montana. They're very chic, very elegant, and are located in a beautiful area that is in the sunniest region of Switzerland. And both have panoramic views of the Alps and the Rhône Valley. As with many other towns in the Alps that year, there was very little snow, and the sun had been shining warmly. Even the frozen lake, where the dogsled racing usually took place, was melting and it wasn't yet Easter.

The mountains were starting to burst into blossom. It seemed as though there were flowers of every colour in every garden, and white and pink blossoms on every tree. The birds were busy and noisy, and you could hear the running water over the rocks as ice melted into the little streams. The overall effect was stunning—the mountains with their glistening snow-covered peaks, the sun shining in a brilliant blue sky, the trees bursting with flowers and new leaves, and everywhere, the grass a bright, eager green. Spring in the mountains was truly beautiful that year.

We found a place to stay, after searching for a day or two, at a *hôtel-résidence* high in the hills. We got a fabulous apartment, overlooking the valley, for a song because the season had been so poor. The window, like a huge wall-size picture, was a changing scene every day, each day more captivating than the one before.

We filled our mornings walking, and Marco played bridge in the afternoons, while I went to the movies (a great delight for me since I never had time before). In the evenings, we

A Journey of a Thousand Miles Begins with a Single Step

discussed, endlessly, articles from Marco's yachting magazines. He had more than a dozen of them and would show me some of the fabulous sailboats that were available. He was still trying to convince me. I still didn't want to be convinced.

'Look how elegant it can be inside a boat,' he ventured, knowing my predilection for elegance.

'Look how cramped it is,' I responded.

'A sailboat, even if it capsizes, won't stay capsized,' he reasoned.

I showed him a picture of one that had.

'There's always the exception,' he conceded, unmoved.

We discussed makes and prices. We studied ads—that is, he studied ads. I looked on despairingly.

'At least try to get involved,' he complained, 'show a little bit of enthusiasm.'

How could I when this whole episode of my life seemed to have a dark shadow hanging over it?

'I'm sorry, Marco, but the thought of the boat terrifies me. We know so little about it; even the vocabulary is different. I don't even know what half the words mean.'

'Well, we'll learn. It's never stopped us before. That's the whole idea.'

The truth is that I was dreading the day we would leave the mountains and head to the Riviera to buy the boat.

'We'll go down just after Easter, that should be a good time,' Marco figured. 'We shouldn't go sooner, the weather's not right and there's not much activity yet.' (Ominously, Good Friday was on 13 April that year.)

But Friday the 13th turned up trumps—for me at least. We woke up, looked out the window and saw that several metres

The Year of Sunshine

of snow had fallen during the night—we were snowed in for three days. I had won a reprieve, three days and counting.

The following week as the weather eased, we had to start driving down to the Riviera. The dreaded moment had finally come.

'You like Alassio,' said Marco. 'We'll start off there.'

He knew me well, and offered me inducements that he seemed to time to keep me happy. Alassio is an ancient Mediterranean town about an hour north of Genoa, with wonderful restaurants along the seafront, elegant boutiques and a pretty port with lots of bars filled with noisy, happy people. The atmosphere always renewed me. My mind went back, nostalgically, to my boutique days when I stayed in Alassio for a short time before continuing to Florence. How I had loved those times, a lifetime ago. But now was now, and we were in the business of buying a boat.

We had decided to take the route through Geneva, and stayed there for a couple of days.

Thirty years before, at the beginning of our marriage, we had worked out of Geneva. They were exciting years and were ten of the best years of our lives. We had driven through Geneva on other trips to the mountains, but hadn't been back to where we lived or worked.

Just for old time's sake, we parked the car outside what was once our company offices. We went to the park opposite, where we knew we would see busy red squirrels scampering across lawns, and running up and down the trees. It was a pretty sight, and a very European one, which I missed. At the gates of the park we both stopped and looked back over the road. The building was old now, weary and ordinary.

A Journey of a Thousand Miles Begins with a Single Step

'So much water under the bridge,' Marco remarked wistfully.

'Mmmm,' I agreed.

During our previous visits to Geneva, we had pretty much always kept to the Montreux side of the lake, but we decided to explore the other side before going south. We discovered a medieval town called Yvoire. It is beautifully restored with a castle, fortifications, and paved streets bordered by a multitude of handicraft shops. There are floral displays everywhere and the colourful little port with sailboats and a small ferry coming and going all add to its charm. The specialty of the area is *filets des perches*. At a lakeside restaurant, we had an incredible meal with our plates piled high with small fillets of perch, deep fried, served with a butter sauce, *pommes frites* and *salade verte* washed down with chilled Chablis, and finally, profiteroles covered with a litre of hot chocolate sauce—delicious.

'It's time to find our boat,' said Marco.

It was time to go. I had avoided it for long enough.

Alassio, first stop.

We installed ourselves in a hotel, and started asking around at the port, but everywhere we tried, we got the same reply.

'It's too late, all the best boats sell in January and February, there's not much left.'

I couldn't believe my ears. Was I to get a permanent stay of execution, I wondered joyously?

But Marco was not daunted.

'That's not possible. I can't believe there's not a boat here for us all up and down the Riviera. We'll try France.'

So the next day we drove to Menton, just over the border, and went to the port. There were a couple of boat agents but only one was open. We described the type of boat we wanted including the requirement for a large bedroom since we had never had a boat before, and I was sure I would feel claustrophobic.

'I know just what you want,' said the agent, 'I'll get my wife to show you something.'

Oh no, please no, I pleaded silently.

But here I was being taken out to a boat that looked dirty and totally forbidding. There was no gangplank so I had to jump across from the quay to the moored boat. I tried not to look scared but my heart was so tight I could hardly breathe, let alone jump.

I'll get you for this. One day, I'll get you, I hissed silently to Marco.

I got across. I had never been aboard a sailboat before.

They opened the door and I peered into the dark, hot, mildew-smelling boat. This is definitely not for me, I said to myself.

Surely Marco didn't have this in mind for the rest of my life? The galley was filthy and somebody had put down a hot saucepan on the counter, such as it was, and burnt a hole almost right through. The upholstery in the main saloon was revolting. The sleeping accommodation was a one-and-a-half size bed and a couple of narrow bunks.

Oh no, I wailed silently, I can't do this.

Marco was sitting with the agent, discussing what could be done by a carpenter and some new upholstery.

I couldn't believe what I was hearing.

I can't do this, I repeated to myself, I can't do this.

'I'll show you another one,' said the agent.

A Journey of a Thousand Miles Begins with a Single Step

She took us over to another run-down dirty boat. 'This one has a huge owner's cabin and bed,' she said, 'You'll like this one.'

This one had a gangplank, but no hand-rails. I had to get across without holding on. I thought I was going to be sick. I felt as if I was walking the plank. In fact, this whole project, to me, was like walking the plank. I couldn't help feeling I was going to die at the end of it.

Again she opened the door to a dark, dank-smelling hothouse. We climbed in, and I asked to see the double cabin first. She took us forward and showed us a bed, which could only be described as a one-and-a-half size bed that ended in a point which you had to crawl into. The ceiling was only three feet high.

Claustrophobia overcame me and I had an overwhelming desire to throw up or be hysterical.

Hysteria won, and I began giggling uncontrollably. I couldn't believe this was happening to me, and I couldn't believe elegant, fussy Marco wanted to live on board something like this.

The interior decor looked as if somebody had collected all the unwanted items from several clean-up campaigns, and installed them. I'm sure they thought they had done a great job, but somehow it wasn't quite where I had envisaged spending the rest of my life.

Where was the sleek dining table with roses that featured in every photograph in Marco's yachting magazines? Where was the polished teak panelling, the designer galley, and the double bed with the satin quilt and still more roses on the dressing table? Where were they?

The Year of Sunshine

Dear God, he can't be going through with this, I tried to reassure myself.

'What are you laughing at?' Marco demanded of me.

'What's so funny?' the agent asked.

'I ... don't think ... this was ... quite ... what I ... expected,' I managed to blurt out.

Marco impatiently ignored me and he returned to his conversation with the agent.

On our way back to the agency, as we walked away from the quay, I glanced back at both boats and caught their names. One was *Punishment* and the other, *Satan*. I shook my head, and it wasn't just the names that bothered me.

It was about this time, racing up and down the A8 *autoroute* between the French and Italian Riviera, looking at ports and boats, that we had a bad experience with our beautiful car. Life has a funny way of telling us things, and I couldn't help but feel there was a meaning in it somewhere.

We were speeding back down to Italy at about 180 kilometres an hour when we heard a funny noise. It seemed to be coming from the front. We slowed down and stopped, ran it up and down slowly, saw nothing, heard nothing, but every time we got back on the road, the noise slowly got worse. We had only just gone through the frontier at Ventimiglia, and had nearly an hour to go to Alassio, leaving the *autostrada* at Albenga.

Marco reasoned that he was better off if he could limp along the *autostrada* to Albenga since it was closer to Alassio, rather than go off at an earlier exit, but much farther away from base.

All the time, he was fuming with frustration and embarrassment as other cars passed us. The ones with youths in

A Journey of a Thousand Miles Begins with a Single Step

them honked their horns at us, hung out of the windows, and made rude signs as they shot past the limping Jaguar.

It must have taken us a good two hours or more between San Remo and Albenga. It got worse and worse, and we lost the brakes.

It was quite dark when we crawled into the pay toll at Albenga.

I stuck my head out of the window and asked the cashier where the nearest phone was to call road assistance. He asked me what was wrong.

'I don't know. There's something funny with the front wheel.' I said.

He glanced down and his eyes opened wide.

'I'm not surprised,' he said. 'It's almost off.'

I got out of the car and looked down at the wheel. It was sitting at an oblique angle to the axle.

I couldn't believe my eyes. I don't know how we hadn't lost the wheel and come to a disastrous end.

'*Dio ti vuole bene*,' he said nodding his head. Literally translated it means, 'God loves you,' but in this case meant 'You're lucky'.

I was counting on it.

A couple of hours later we climbed into the cabin of the tow truck beside the driver. I looked out of the back window at our dream car being towed along inelegantly with its front wheels and bonnet suspended in the air, and wondered how long my luck could hold out.

Chapter 3

Destiny Unknown

'I think I've found it! Come and see.' He was so excited he could hardly contain himself.

I rounded the corner to the port, and there it was in the sparkling water—sun drenching its decks and light beams dancing around it. It was a 42-foot ketch—romantic, light and airy. Even as a non-enthusiast, I was impressed.

There could be no boat more appropriate to a pair of novices in a situation like ours than: *Destiny Unknown*. The name was right and it had a FOR SALE sign.

We went on board and the owners showed us around. It was clean and big and felt like an apartment. After what we'd seen so far—small boats, scruffy boats, smelly boats, boats with cabins smaller than closets—this boat was paradise.

We explained to the owners, a Dutch couple called Pieter and Stella, that we knew nothing about boats, and asked if they would stay on board and teach us as part of the deal.

The Year of Sunshine

'Of course,' they agreed, nodding enthusiastically. (Actually they didn't speak very much English, but Marco didn't seem to think that mattered.) Here, surely, was a heaven-sent opportunity.

The price was a little higher than we anticipated, but perhaps we could negotiate.

We were excited and anxious for different reasons. I, because after all the boats we had seen, I felt reasonably safe on this one, but sick to my stomach at the thought of living on it. Marco was relieved that I had finally 'taken' to a boat instead of stubbornly opposing it, but felt perhaps it was too soon; after all, he hadn't yet seen every single boat available.

Up to this point in my life, I had never owned a pair of jeans or flat shoes, never having had the need or the desire to wear them. I bought my first pair of jeans, a denim shirt and docksiders, as a statement of begrudgingly warming to the idea. Besides, that's what all the Riviera yachties were wearing and they looked great. The jeans were just a sign of softening, not surrender.

I kept the long red nails though—I wasn't giving in totally. Before leaving Australia, I'd had lunch with a barrister client of mine who had become a close friend. When I told her we were going sailing, she confided, 'Oh, I don't like sailing! You break your nails.' She wasn't wrong. This was yet to come, together with the crumpled T-shirts and shorts, bare feet, and cold showers.

'Let's ask around to check if the price is right.' Marco had set his mind on a certain figure and wanted to make sure it was within budget. We also needed to know a few other things. Did the boat have osmosis, a fibreglass disease commonly called fibreglass cancer, which is troublesome and expensive to remove. A dry hull inspection is needed to detect this. And there were the practicalities, such as how we would get an Australian flag and Australian registration.

The first thing we needed to do was to find someone whom we could trust to give a proper appraisal of the boat. Start at the top, Italian Marco always says, a believer of the it's-not-what-you-know-but-who-you-know approach. We sought out someone from the yacht club, Signor Baraldi, who kindly agreed to come and have a look.

He came on board, a small, old man with a brown leathery face and cheeky eyes.

'I'll need to discuss it with a friend of mine in Rapallo. He's a boat agent and I respect his opinion,' he told us wisely. 'I'll let you know tomorrow.'

We thought this was a good idea, and waited impatiently for his return the next day.

Baraldi walked up and down on deck with a certain importance, an air of knowing, and stated imperialistically, 'My friend said the price was too high.'

The owners, also there for the appraisal, looked dejected. Pieter ran his fingers through his hair in frustration. He had explained earlier that he had spent so much on the boat, made several additions, and wanted to cover his costs. We gathered from talking to them that they were getting short of money, since they were staying in the part of the port without electricity, and were leading a very Spartan life. He said that he had a back problem, that's why he was selling. Talking to Stella, I also found out that she was a reluctant sailor, like me, and I believe she was exerting pressure on him. They were obviously in a hurry to sell, and a new price was agreed. Baraldi winked at Marco.

'Now we must check for osmosis,' said Baraldi. 'You can use my *cantiere* (shipyard).'

We were up early the next morning and Pieter took us on the boat so we could motor to the *cantiere*. I have never seen a more complicated manoeuvre. We set off in fairly calm water, but when we got there about 40 minutes later, the current was so strong that Pieter couldn't get the boat into the right position for the boat lift.

The sea had become *un peu agité*, as they say on the weather forecasts, with increasingly choppy waves lapping against the hull. I got the distinct feeling they wanted to devour us. We tried to go in, but couldn't, so went out again, tried to go in again, then out. After several attempts, we finally did it. Oh God, I thought, I hope we never have to do this on our own. My feelings of self-worth were crushed by my inadequacy and, again, I doubted whether I would ever be able to cope with the sailing of any boat. I had no affinity with sailing and, of course, I lacked *la voglia* (the want to) without which little is possible.

'We'll learn.' Marco told me every time I voiced my opinion.

We eventually got in and were hauled up with us all aboard. It was a good ten feet high up on the sling. I asked Baraldi when it would be finished. He thought that afternoon.

'But that doesn't mean you can take the boat back out, the weather might be too rough.'

'What about Pieter and Stella?' I was concerned for them.

'Well, they can either go to a hotel or *pensione*, or sleep on board if they want,' he said.

Destiny Unknown

Stella had a pet dog on board which she wouldn't leave, so they slept right up there—slung ten feet high. When I saw Stella next morning I asked her how they had managed. She pointed to a bucket and shrugged her shoulders.

When we saw Baraldi, he told us all was well, and that he had painted some anti-fouling solution over a couple of parts that needed it, and that was 700,000 lire please. We were able to leave in calm water, much to my relief.

That was the first of many hundreds of dollars we spent on 'the boat'. Whoever said, 'A boat is a big hole in the water that you throw your money into', knew what he (or she) was talking about.

Now Pieter started teaching us a few of the things we needed to know.

We would meet on the boat at an appointed time. I had my notebook and pen, and took appropriate notes. Let's start with the knots, we understood him to say, since he was holding two pieces of rope and offered one to each of us. I picked the knots up quickly remembering my girl guide proficiency badges of a thousand years ago, but Marco couldn't tell one end of rope from the other, and had great difficulty following the examples and ended up with his arms in knots, and us doubled up laughing at his antics. His attempts were accompanied by '*Si, più o meno*', (Yes, I've got it ... more or less).

We went through the Dutch chart of buoys, but since Pieter didn't know half the names in English, we could only guess at what that half meant.

I was, by now, painfully aware that it could all be starting soon. Marco was not listening to me; he was having too much fun. Had I run out of reprieves? In desperation, I began communicating silently with whoever would listen. Oh God, please save me from certain disaster.

We had many long conversations with Baraldi at the port. We would sit outside the yacht club at the little tables set in the sun, sipping our Camparis, surrounded by people in striped T-shirts and navy shorts, talking and laughing loudly. We discussed how little we knew and how gadget-oriented we were, hoping the gadgets would make up for our lack of knowledge and take the hard work out of sailing for us and he kept saying, 'You don't need a sailboat, you need a motorboat.'

'Yes,' I agreed with him, 'I would prefer a motorboat.'

'No,' insisted Marco, 'I want a sailboat.'

I had occasion to phone Baraldi about some advice and again he told me, 'Signora, listen to me. Try and persuade your husband to get a motorboat instead.'

What was I letting myself in for? I had hated the idea from the beginning, and had allowed myself to be persuaded into thinking it wasn't so bad. What did he know that I didn't? Loads, obviously.

What could I do? We had already spent 700,000 lire on the boat and we didn't even own it yet. I had made the decision to see this summer through, whatever it brought, and I would do it.

Registering the boat in our names was a complicated rigmarole. Pieter had no idea and couldn't help at all, and certainly his lack of English would have kept us from finding out. But nobody else seemed to know. The complications arose because we were in Italy, the boat was registered in

Destiny Unknown

Holland, and we were Australian. We couldn't keep Dutch registration because we weren't Dutch, that much he knew. We couldn't have Italian registration because the boat would have to be imported to Italy and import duty paid, and besides, we weren't resident in Italy.

We called the Australian Consulate in Milan about getting Australian registration, but they didn't know, and referred us to Rome. The Rome consul would find out and let us know. They faxed back pages and pages of instructions that looked awesome, and were full of marine words we didn't recognise. We shook our heads.

We also had to confirm that there were no encumbrances on the boat, but this, Pieter kept pointing out, was clearly stamped on the back of the registration papers. However, we wanted it checked and confirmed.

This was getting more complicated, and I spent hours on the phone trying to get it sorted out. We asked everybody we could think of, but it was too hard for everyone. We called a *notaio* (notary)—it wasn't in the jurisdiction of notaries, I was told. We called ship agents—everyone had a different version. We searched up and down the coast and finally came across a boat agent in St Laurent du Var, just beyond Nice Airport, who said he could do it for us for a fee, but in the end, he couldn't work it out either.

Then there were the bill of sale and exchange documents, which we wanted in English and Pieter wanted in Dutch, so we tried to find an Italian lawyer who could do the transaction in English and Dutch. You've got to be kidding, we were told. So we proceeded to look for one on the French Riviera, since we knew there were some American lawyers there who worked in several languages. In addition, Marco wanted to pay with a bank cheque, as was the habit in Australia for such a large purchase, but Pieter wanted us to transfer the money to his account in Holland, because of the fees involved with a bank cheque, then he would sign the boat over to us.

'Let's abide by the lawyer,' said Marco. In principle Pieter agreed, but still insisted on a transfer saying he knew this would be acceptable.

We all drove up to Nice in our car to see the English and Dutch-speaking lawyer, each with our own secret thoughts. We turned up to the appointment only to find that he had been kept at a conference out of town. Did they know of another lawyer with the same qualifications? Yes, at the other end of town. We all traipsed over there, to be kept waiting an hour longer while he finished with another client.

When he could finally see us, we went in, sat down and told our story. After listening attentively, with a question thrown in here and there, the lawyer said to Pieter, 'I would never advise a client to transfer funds in a case like this, and we certainly must do searches for encumbrances.'

'But I don't agree to this,' said Pieter angrily, 'and I don't want it done this way.'

'Well then,' Marco shot back, 'you can keep your boat!'

We apologised to the lawyer, he said something about it being a 'non-agreement' and we walked out, and that was that.

The atmosphere was frigid in the car on the return journey to the port, with not a word uttered by anyone for the whole hour and a half. I hardly dared to glance at the two men but couldn't resist, Marco beside me, Pieter behind. Both men stared stonily ahead, their jaws set in stubborn lines.

But I spoke silent volumes. 'Thank you, thank you, thank you.' I said to whoever was watching over me.

When I phoned Baraldi to tell him the deal had fallen through and I was calling to say goodbye and thank you, he said, '*Signora, Dio ti ha voluto bene,*' (Signora, God looked after you).

And I smiled a secret smile, raised my eyes towards heaven, winked, and said silently, God, I owe you one.

Chapter 4

Searching the Italian Riviera

We each had mixed emotions about the deal falling through. I was relieved because I had another reprieve, but I knew Marco would keep searching. Marco tortured himself wondering if he had acted too hastily, as I had warmed to the idea but was now stone cold again. However, he was also relieved because he had known too little about the transaction, which had been very complicated.

'Well,' said he, true to form, 'I shall search the whole of the Italian and French Riviera, and if I still don't find it, I shall go to Spain, and if I still don't find it, I shall search Northern France, and then England, and then Holland if I have to.'

My heart sank because I knew he would.

Oh my God, I thought, this could take months and months. I had now been away two and a half months. I missed my daughters and they missed me. I was sick of the car, boats, ports and hotel rooms. I had had enough. In my opinion I had really tried.

'I'm sorry, Marco, but I'm going home,' I said.

'You can't go home, I need you. Come on, Angel,' he cajoled, *ti amo.*'

He enveloped me in his arms and kissed me. He always knew the right thing to say and do.

'But I don't like this,' I pouted.

'Of course you do, you only think you don't,' he replied typically, stroking my hair affectionately then contouring my shoulder, arm and body, making my resolve weaken.

'Oh, all right.' Sighing, I relented reluctantly. I would achieve nothing if I walked off now anyway. How bad could it be, after all? Just a few more ports and a few more boats, I would have to do what I would have to do if it would make him happy. I resigned myself to a few more months.

'Well,' said Marco, 'we'll start by going down through Portofino to Cecina and further south if we have to.' (Another of Marco's well-timed inducements as Portofino, he knew, was another favourite of mine.)

We headed south with our first port of call Rapallo. It looked glorious with flowers everywhere—brilliant red hibiscus; pale blue drifts of the plumbago; purple, red and orange bougainvillea. The flowers covered ancient walls and the sides of houses, and spilled out of roadside planters.

We stopped at our favourite trattoria, *Da Alfredo* in Santa Marguerita di Ligure, just after Portofino. It is set back on the coastal road, which follows the sea in great sweeps and curves. The road winds up the hill, past graceful old villas, with cypresses and flower-filled gardens, all lit up at night. It is sublimely pretty. *Da Alfredo* is on this road amongst a half-dozen other restaurants and trattorias. Extra tables are set out on the pavement, covered by an awning, and the atmosphere is truly great.

Nobody makes *antipasto di mare* (marinated calamari and baby octopus) and *spaghetti al cartoccio* (spaghetti cooked in seafood sauce in foil) like Alfredo. The trattoria's popularity is proven by the ever-present queue for tables.

Marco, true to his Italian heritage, is a gourmand, a connoisseur of food and plenty of it. He can tell a great restaurant based purely on its *profumo*. If in doubt, he will tell me to wait outside while he walks through the restaurant as though he owns it, picking up the scent and glancing from side to side as he surveys the plates already served. He will then either motion for me to get going by covertly signalling the Italian 'get going' gesture or come out smiling. He might have the *padrone*, with him and he will often have made a brief but lasting impression as someone very important in the food industry. At this point, we will get the best table and top service.

Luckily, I could never eat the amounts of food that he could so I managed to stay fairly slim, although it was a source of constant amazement that I did. Perhaps it was just keeping up with all his crazy adventures that did it.

We stayed at a simple *pensione*—it was cheap and old. The bedroom had high ceilings, a prefabricated bathroom that had been added in the last ten years, a great dark cupboard with no coat hangers, and the bed had a dip in the middle. It reminded me of places we had stayed at 30 years ago, but it was all we could find.

The Year of Sunshine

We had been told that we wouldn't find accommodation anywhere in Italy because of the World Cup and, they said, your lovely car will be vandalised. I made a conscious decision to enjoy what I could while I could.

Rapallo turned up nothing. We spent hours and hours looking at boats, wandering up and down the quays and pontoons, talking to agents. We had noticed a few people with small foldable bikes and remarked how useful they would be when we bought the boat.

We were halfway through May, and the weather was fabulous that year. The sun was already hot and we were getting tanned just walking up and down looking at the boats.

We searched the next two ports, Chiaveri and Lavagna, which were practically side by side. Up and down the pontoons we walked, more agents, more boats to see, everything left was either too expensive or no good. It was tiring, and I talked Marco into buying the fold-up bikes sooner rather than later, so that we wouldn't have to walk everywhere. This was one of the best decisions I ever made. We rode everywhere on our bikes. I had not been on a bike since childhood, and I had forgotten what fun they could be. We would fold them up and put them in the back of our car, and get them out at every place we stopped, causing a small sensation each time. I don't know why, maybe because the wheels are small, and they have an almost clownish look, but they are so practical.

There was an air of excitement everywhere because of the World Cup. Football to Italians is like their food, wine and love. They are wildly passionate about it. Italians are noisy and chaotic, and they have a wonderful passion for life, which is difficult to find anywhere else. It is most definitely contagious. I was starting to enjoy this, and had fantasies about us not finding a boat at all, but staying in Italy for the summer, which I would happily do.

Next port, Viareggio. It's popular with Italians and tourists alike, famous for its long sweeping beach, hundreds of *bagni* (sectioned off areas of beach with deck chairs for hire) and a fantastic promenade full of the best boutiques, gelaterie and nightclubs. It is another of my favourites. It was one of the first places Marco brought me to after we eloped 30 years ago.

I love being in Viareggio—tearing along the autostrada to get there, having a macchiato at every stop and listening to Mango, Minghi or Pavarotti singing at the top of their lungs is a part of the joy.

Since we were in the Viareggio–Lucca area, Marco wanted to look up an old school friend with whom he had lost touch. His sister also knew him and told us where we could find him. In a small place like Lucca, the inhabitants rarely move out and pretty well everyone knows each other or, if they don't, they can direct you to someone who does.

We arrived at the friend's home and Daniele's joy at seeing Marco again was unimaginable. He and his wife welcomed us and hugged us both. The two men hugged each other and laughed and laughed and, as the words spilled out of them, they hardly drew breath.

'Where have you been, what crazy things have you been getting up to lately?'

'Do you remember the time we roller-skated from Lucca

to Pisa? We were crazy then, weren't we? How old were we, fourteen? Yes, we must have been thirteen or fourteen.'

'And how about when you used to climb up to my window when I couldn't come out. You must have been ten. How mad we were. Where did you meet your wife? London? Oh my God, what were you doing there? Marco, you never change. What are you doing now? Sydney. Australia. A sailboat—*accidenti!*'

Out came the wine and we sat on their terrace and they talked and talked, including me in their conversation—their enthusiasm was overwhelming.

'You must come to dinner tonight, we are having some friends over. Some you will know already from years back, they will love to see you again. You must come, say you will. Yes, you will, won't you?'

It was a statement rather than a question, and of course we did go, and of course we had the most wonderful time, eating and drinking, talking and laughing until late into the night.

The next day we were invited to their daughter's house in the countryside, just outside Lucca for a lunchtime feast, al fresco. The countryside was magnificent with sunflower fields and olive groves and the heat hung heavy in the air. Two large tables were set up under big, leafy trees in a huge garden dotted with olive trees. To the side of it was a field where fruit and vegetables were grown. The table laden with food and wine was a beautiful sight. A bowl of big, plump, bright red tomatoes (which incidentally are so flavoursome as to be heavenly), next to another bowl brimming to the top with creamy soft mozzarella, a bunch of fresh basil and a bottle of thick, green olive oil. Platters of chicken done in rosemary and wine and that smelled and tasted exquisite were next to a plate of veal roasted in milk. Plates of *crostini* (similar to bruschette) were brought out covered either in tomato, homemade olive paste, or minced chicken livers cooked with eggs and brandy. A huge dish of *fagioli all'uccelletto* (fresh borlotti beans cooked in tomato and garlic sauce) was brought out in Marco's honour since it is one of his favourites. Lastly, enormous loaves of Italian bread accompanied by bottles of local red and white wine bought from the *contadini*, and several bottles of *acqua minerale* (mineral water), were placed in the centre and we were ready to sit down.

We must have been ten at the table including Daniele's sister and Emilia's brother, and their children and grandchildren—their laughter and talk noisy, the food unforgettable. After that came the platters of watermelon, bowls of fruit and huge tubs of gelato. And then the coffee and *vin santo* (dessert wine). We could hardly move from the table after that meal, but we found sun chairs and placed them in the shade and dozed in the afternoon sun. It was a truly delectable afternoon.

The next day was Sunday, so we invited Daniele and Emilia to lunch at a restaurant we had heard about high up in Garfagnana, the mountains an hour or so away from Lucca. Driving through the Garfagnana hills during the heat of the day, the narrow winding road shaded by trees, is beautifully cool. Most restaurants up there have huge covered terraces and to eat on the terrace al fresco, looking down on the panoramic views of green rolling hills, is spectacular. The

The Year of Sunshine

food is also out of this world. The area has many specialties and the restaurateurs are masters at creating exquisitely delicious dishes. This restaurant, like several in this area, served a fixed price menu. First comes several rounds of antipasti (chef's selection), then two or three *paste*—usually one with porcini mushrooms, one with a meat sauce, any combination of beef, veal and rabbit, and one ravioli dish (my favourite is spinach and ricotta ravioli served with a butter sauce and sage leaves). After that comes a choice of meat dishes. *Arista di maiale* (roast pork), *rosticciana* (barbecued meat) and maybe *pollo e coniglio fritti* (fried chicken and rabbit pieces) all served with a combination of vegetables, with or without sauce, or mixed salad with rocket and tomatoes. As this point I usually need a digestive, so I have a *caffè corretto* (espresso with Fernet Branca in it), but Marco keeps going. There might be two or three desserts, maybe tiramisu or *torta della nonna* (a delicious light sponge cake with a custard cream filling topped with sliced almonds) and always *macedonia* (fruit salad) and gelato. Finally, *vin santo* is served together with *cantucci* (almond biscuits) which, incidentally, are dipped into the glass of wine. Coffee is optional.

We said goodbye to our newfound friends with promises to visit next time we were down there.

It is really astonishing how quickly the day goes in Italy. At lunch, I was talking to Emilia and her daughter about how everything seems to revolve around food. At twelve-thirty, everything closes for lunch and re-opens at three-thirty or four. This cuts your day into two short bursts. If you get up at eight-thirty or nine, have breakfast and tidy up, ready to go out by ten-thirty, you have two hours in which to do everything before the shops close otherwise you have to do it in the afternoon. Then everyone has lunch and a nap and you get ready to go out again around four but before you know it, it's seven and time to go home and make dinner. It's one long round of eating, sleeping and cooking, which at first I found strange and almost a waste of time but now it seems so natural and so basically gratifying.

We had a fabulous time in Viareggio. There must be a vortex or something there that has a positive effect on me. I felt so happy, in love and young again. It is really a good tonic as I always come away feeling reborn and wonderful. The countryside is mystical and magical, and the people so warm, generous and kind, that my faith in human nature is restored.

You definitely won't find accommodation in Viareggio, we were told, so decided to play it safe and stay at Marina di Massa, one of the little towns north of Viareggio. The climate gets hotter the further south you go and you get a wonderful change in the scenery. The *pineta* (maritime pine forests) just next to the beach provide divinely cooled shade from the midday sun, and a slice of chilled watermelon (sold at kiosks in the *pineta*) is the most delicious thing when you're hot and dying of thirst.

The promenades were still fairly empty, although holiday-makers were starting to arrive. The air was vibrant with expectation of the forthcoming football matches. Everybody was talking about them. There were larger-than-life, cube-football-player statues everywhere in the Italian colours of green, white and red. Italian flags were flying from anything that had a post or window to attach them to. Every TV was tuned into sports channels.

The Year of Sunshine

We visited the ports, without success, but had fun riding our bikes up and down the promenades, taking lunch, then having an afternoon nap in the car in the shade of the *pineta* with the seats laid back and the windows wound right down. A truly indulgent thing to do.

It was time to continue, down to Cecina. Marco had a cousin there who sailed boats and he wanted to ask him a few questions. Nearing Marina di Cecina on the coast, the scenery became even more rustic and the vegetation a wonderful combination of spiky cactus and coastal trees including the graceful fronds of the grey-green tamarix, the phoenix palm, the ever-present Italian cypress and the *pini maritime* in their verdant abundance.

The burning sun shone from a hot blue sky, and there was a lovely sense of laissez-faire.

Gelato and cappuccino were the order of the day. The further south we got, the more 'Italian' it became. It was no longer obviously touristy, but true, full-flavoured mamma's pasta, garlic and *salsa Napolitana*.

We were also now deep in the heart of the Italian gestures, like the fingertips of one hand all being brought together and being shaken to and fro which means, more or less, 'What are you doing?' or 'What do you want?' or just 'Are you mad?' We got this sign several times as we overtook trucks, from the driver coming towards us in the opposite direction. Then there's the one with the fingers and palm flattened in a straight line and the index finger side knocked against the forehead which means 'Are you crazy?' We got this one too, when we overtook, and of course they all thought a woman was driving because the steering wheel in

Searching the Italian Riviera

Italy is on the opposite side to English cars. Had they noticed a man driving I am sure there would have been no signs, just admiration.

Oh Italy, I love you, but you are so chauvinistic.

There was a lovely incident when Marco, driving along, started chuckling. I asked him what was funny. He said he had seen a couple on the roadside and had understood what they had said to each other without hearing a word. The youth had gestured to the girl to go down a cliff trail to the beach. She had pointed to herself, pointed down the cliff, pointed to her high-heeled shoes, made the gesture with the fingertips, and then knocked her forehead with her flattened palm. Marco translated, 'me, down there, with these shoes, what do you take me for? Are you crazy?'

It is not necessary to speak Italian; you only have to know the sign language.

I was beginning to love being back in Italy again and found it was working its old magic on me.

It was in Cecina that we had our first night interrupted by the football.

We had found a beautiful old *pensione* set back from the coast road quite near the cool *pineta*, in a quiet part of town, or so we thought.

That night, after driving for hours, we had gone to bed early only to be woken soon after eleven by honking horns and a parade of cars driving round and round, accompanied by yells and jubilant shouts. It went on for a good while, and I wondered if Marco knew what it could be all about.

'It's probably only football fans,' came the sleepy reply.

It was, and Italy had won the first round.

The Year of Sunshine

Throughout the next days, whenever there was another match, the whole scene was repeated again, with parades of cars full of Italy's exuberant youth honking horns, yelling and shouting joyously, and leaning out of car windows with flags and banners. It was certainly adding zest and colour to our trip.

In Cecina, Marco's cousin was delighted to see him again after so many years, and extremely impressed with what he intended to do, saying that he wished he had the courage to do it too. He suggested we go to Punta Ala, another port further south. So into the car again, for another few hours to a beautiful port, clean and organised, but with no boats for sale.

We walked around the quay, the sun was hot and intense, the sea blue and lazy. Here I saw a man climb a ladder to the top of the sea-wall, calling softly in a loving voice, '*Tesoro*, (treasure), darling, my beautiful baby, did you miss me? I told you I would be back, that I wouldn't be long. Here I am, my darling.'

Intrigued, I watched. I just didn't know what to expect and a bird, with a string attached to its leg, came into view and jumped on his shoulder, and appeared to love him as much as he loved her.

'Well, that's pretty much it,' said Marco. 'Time to go north. We should try Marseilles and Toulon, then cross Spain and go for La Rochelle and St Malo. OK?'

Chapter 5

Searching France and Spain

We back-tracked again, and stayed at Alassio for the night, then proceeded along the coast towards France. We stopped at San Remo, to see a couple more agents.

At one of the ports where we had stopped previously, we had been seen two quite likely boats; both had just been bought and the owners were living on board.

One was a 39-foot Contest in beautiful condition. As I had admired it from the quay, the owner, an Italian, had very kindly offered to show us on board; it was really beautiful. Luxuriously and tastefully appointed, it was ideal for living and cruising. The other was a Westerly, also very beautiful, not quite as luxurious, but harmonious and comfortable. Of the two I preferred the Contest but both were great.

The Year of Sunshine

We were invited for coffee on board both boats. Everybody was so friendly. This I liked.

Marco was visibly unwinding and happy with his adventures so far. The stress was disappearing from his face and his tan accentuated his good looks. I was warming to the Mediterranean magic and feeling a great deal more accommodating.

However, I was still half-in, half-out. I loved being there with him, but I would occasionally be overwhelmed by emotion. Nostalgia for my girls, Sydney and the life I had left behind. Anxiety about the promises I had made to myself and preoccupation for whatever was in the future. I would stare out of the car window and all of a sudden burst into tears. He would pull over and hold me, concerned. Sometimes he would be sympathetic, and sometimes angry.

'Angel, are you really so unhappy?'

'I just miss the girls so much.' At times like this I felt as though my heart would break, it was aching so much.

'Me too, but as soon as we get the boat they can come over.'

This didn't really appease my battered soul as much as he would have liked.

He would utter a frustrated sigh.

'Come on, Angel, we can only do this together.'

I know it hurt him to cause me pain, but I also knew he was on a mission, and I know he truly believed that it was going to be good for both of us. I was still really not convinced.

It was not that I regretted my decision to come with him. I was happy about that. It was giving me a chance to put things right between us, which was desperately important to me. But at what cost to me and to my self-esteem. I had

Searching France and Spain

enjoyed my role of decision-maker in my business, but I also knew that Marco liked control. While I had my boutique, and even when I helped him out in his office, I had the control. At home, it was silently agreed that I would take care of the domestic side, plus selected items, and he the rest. But here the situation was such that there was no control for me, only submission, and this is what I had been afraid of before my decision to come with him. 'Me captain, you crew'—it said it all.

I felt manipulated, and I wasn't sure I was going to be able to live with that for the rest of my life. Retirement with a man telling me what to do all the time would drive me crazy, I knew. I told myself I could wait a bit longer to see how it developed when we got the boat, perhaps things would be different.

Then again, it was one of the things I loved about him when I first met him—his ability to make decisions quickly and act upon them. I found him irresistible when he did this. Often infuriating, but always irresistible.

Marco had, literally, swept me off my feet. Two weeks after we met, he was at my office door with tickets from London to the Continent for us to leave the next day.

My beloved father died a week after I met Marco. I had been devastated and cancelled all my plans. I wanted to leave but felt I ought to stay, even though there was no longer anything keeping me in England. I had stayed for my father who always asked me not to leave him every time I talked about going overseas.

'Do it for me' he always said, after I protested that I had to go, that I was unhappy at home, that Mother made my life

The Year of Sunshine

impossible. But I would agree to stay a bit longer, just for him, only for him.

Mother and I did not share a close relationship. We shared nothing, really, except a mutual dislike for each other. I suppose I hoped she would reach out for me in her pain, but she did not need anyone. She was a loner, and fiercely independent until the end of her ninety-five years. However, I still felt obliged to put my plans on hold but was in no condition to make a decision. Marco had made the decision for me, and whisked me away to Italy where he and his family cared for me and made everything right. That decision had been the most important decision of my life. My life would never be the same. He had made it for me, and I would always thank him for that.

The agent at San Remo said he knew of a Contest in our price range. Marco was ecstatic. We were getting closer. My heart grew small again. It was all right getting on board somebody else's boat and admiring it, it was another thing to possess our own.

'But,' said the agent enigmatically, 'you must follow me, because I am not telling you where it is, otherwise you will go on your own and I will lose my commission.' Intrigued, we arranged to meet him the next morning at the Nice toll on the *autoroute* since we had to get the car fixed first at the Jaguar dealer there. We exchanged descriptions of our cars and agreed on a time.

'How long will it take to get there?' I had asked.

'Oh, about an hour or so.' He wasn't giving anything away.

We thought this was all a bit mysterious, but this was the way he wanted it, and we were obliged to follow. We met up with him and started following. We passed all the exits on the *autoroute* that we knew led to ports. We drove on and on. We finally came off the exit at Le Muy, but there was still another half an hour on another road. We were seeing signs for Port Grimaud, Cogolin and St Tropez. We had been driving now for two and a half hours and it was getting boring. He started slowing and pulled into what appeared to be a private resort and I could see we were entering an incredible looking place. The sign said 'Port Grimaud'.

I don't think I have ever seen anything quite like it.

Started in 1966 and continued through to the 1980s, it was a Provençal village with groups of terraced fishermen's houses, lining seven kilometres of canals around long islands joined together by numerous bridges whose varied architecture made this unique village, which was also known as the Provençal Venice. It was all done in Mediterranean pastels with purple and orange bougainvillea growing everywhere, creeping vines and flowers growing up the walls, and over canal bridges. The shops and restaurants were charming with their striped awnings, adding colour and gaiety to the place, and tables outside had matching coloured tablecloths. Sailboats and motor yachts were moored in the canals, which ran along in the front of the houses. Most houses had a little garden with lawn and trees and flowers, each uniquely individual, but overall part of a great mosaic. It was awe-inspiring. I made a mental note to come back and explore.

We were taken to a Contest dealer, and ushered aboard a small runabout and motored through the canals and under bridges to where three Contests were moored. We climbed aboard the first one. My heart sank. This wasn't like the one we had seen, the layout was completely different, and it wasn't in anywhere near the condition of the other one. The second Contest was older, and the third newer by several thousand dollars.

Marco and I stared glumly at each other across the little runabout taking us back to the car, for different reasons. He, because he thought we had finally found his dream boat, and I because I didn't know how many more thousands of kilometres I could stand in the car before we found his dream boat.

'Well, that's it,' said Marco for the second time. 'Tomorrow we push on to Toulon and Marseilles.'

In fact, we didn't go to Toulon or Marseilles, but decided, impulsively, that we should to go to Andorra via Perpignan, cross Spain, and go directly to Northern France—Marco thought La Rochelle and St Malo would be best.

We hadn't been to Andorra before so were interested in seeing it. Andorra is a little duty-free principality in the Pyrenees between France and Spain. We arrived in the capital, Andorra La Vella, around five as the weather was starting to close in and it was getting cold.

'Finally I can have some *tapas*.' Marco was already savouring the thought.

'Let's book into a hotel and then look for a restaurant.'

Easier said than done.

We drove up the main street of the town, which I can only describe as a little, old and grey skiing village in its smallness and narrow winding streets, with crowded bazaar-type shops everywhere—looking like Hong Kong but without the junks and bright lights. There were no rooms available, but even if

Searching France and Spain

there had been, we would not have been able to park our car in the street or even on the pavement, it was so narrow.

We had been driving for many hours and my back was aching. It also ached from the change in the weather. I was not happy.

'Don't worry, I'll find you something,' consoled Marco, drawing into a square in front of the tourist office.

'What are you going to do, magic up a hotel and some parking?' I asked sarcastically.

'Trust me,' he said, for the umpteenth time on this trip.

Sometimes I underestimate my husband, and this was one of those times. He came back to the car with a smile on his face.

'I promised I'd find you something,' said he, 'and I did. The tourist office tells me there's a hotel further up the mountains, which is not too expensive, and they will have a room for us.'

He was right. About half an hour's drive up the mountains in the very old part of Andorra, there was a very new, very pretty hotel, looking totally out of place with its almost Swiss chalet appearance amongst the ancient neglected buildings of the old town.

By the time we got settled in, it was close to eight o'clock and raining hard, so we opted to eat there, and Marco agreed to find his *tapas* the next day.

We had decided to stay a few days to give me a rest from the car, but the weather was wet and cold, and the food disappointing, being neither Spanish nor French, so we left on the third morning.

As we came down from the mountain, we left the clouds and rain behind. A vast expanse of flat, dry landscape

The Year of Sunshine

opened up before us. We drove for hours across the plains. We drove through the occasional little town, and past the occasional castle. It was hot now, hot and dry and flat. Around four in the afternoon, we arrived in Pamplona, intending to stay the night there. Considering its reputation for wild parties when the bulls are let loose in the streets, we anticipated something quite different. Instead of a little town bursting with life, energy and Spanish zest, we found a sleepy little town where everything was old and grey and dusty, with washing hanging out of the windows or across the narrow streets. I didn't like it. Nor did Marco.

'San Sebastian is only about an hour or so from here,' he said. 'And it's on the coast. It'll be much nicer.'

So we drove on to San Sebastian and arrived around five-thirty. It was much prettier, and had plenty of hotels. We started looking for a room.

'Sorry, booked out.' 'Sorry, full.' 'It's the weekend and everyone is full.'

I had heard this tune before.

'Now what?' I asked.

'Let's ask a local.'

We stopped a couple of people in the street.

'Fuenterrabia's your best bet,' they told us in Spanish. 'You won't find anything else around here, and it's the next town anyway.'

We drew up to a dear little town, so clean and pretty. There were two hotels here, we were told. One was fully booked. One had a room.

'I hope the room is quiet.' I said to the young man at the desk, half hoping and half asking. I desperately needed a good night's sleep. My back was aching after so many hours in the car. We'd been touring for three months and it was beginning to tell on me.

In Europe, it can quite difficult to find a quiet hotel. The traffic goes on and on all night. It quietens down somewhat after one in the morning and starts up again around four. I know because I have spent many nights awakened by the traffic. Once again, I thought nostalgically of Australia and my apartment where the only sounds were the waves and wind.

'Well,' said the desk clerk, 'that side of the building is not bad, because it is on the street. The other side would be worse because it overlooks the *plaza* where all the restaurants and bars are and it's Saturday night, so it will be noisy.'

At three I was still awake from the traffic, the people thronging the streets, the noise and music from the bars. I could stand it no longer. In a fit of rage, I got up, grabbed my pillows and the bedcover we had thrown on a chair, threw them into the bathtub, took a couple of sleeping tablets, closed the bathroom door tightly against the noise, and slept in the tub to the sound of flushing toilets, dreaming that they were waves breaking.

Next morning, we were back on the *autoroute* to La Rochelle. By now, the weather was cooling down considerably. We'd been used to the 30 degree days of the Riviera; this was something new and unwelcome. We had cut down our luggage from three suitcases to one by bringing only necessities (we left two cases at the hotel in Alassio) and because it had been so hot in Italy and the South of France, we had kept to light summer clothing. I had allowed myself

The Year of Sunshine

the luxury of my leather jacket, thank goodness, against Marco's wishes.

'You won't need that,' he had said, disbelieving that I might get cold.

La Rochelle was pretty, and very western France with the effect quite different to that of the Mediterranean coast. The houses had grey rooftops, and the Atlantic was grey and choppy. We visited more agents, up and down the port.

'Nothing here,' they said, 'you'd be better to try Southampton or Port Hamble.'

We pushed on to St Malo with more grey rooftops, but made delightful by the sailboats in port, the colourful restaurants and flowers everywhere. It was even colder now. There were English people everywhere, because St Malo was connected by ferry to a number of English ports.

'No boats,' they told us, 'try England.'

We tried to get the night ferry, but it was fully booked, so we reserved places on the first available one the next day, after spending a cold night at an apartment we came across by chance while looking for a hotel room.

My heart was heavy as we stood on deck while the ferry was drawing into Southampton. Black clouds hung low in the sky, everything was grey and dismal-looking, and it was very cold with that biting chill wind that I knew so well from my youth. I flashed back to my childhood, and the torrential downpours on the two-mile walk to school, with soaking-wet socks and shoes worn all day which seemed to turn to ice from the freezing wind, and the hacking bronchitis that accompanied me through most of January. I have always hated England's weather.

Searching France and Spain

'Come on,' said Marco, putting his arms around me and giving me a hug, 'the sooner we find our boat, the sooner we can leave.'

The boat. The cold wind. The black clouds. The grey sea. I wanted to cry.

Marco had ambitiously suggested we sail the boat ourselves from England across the Channel to France. I wanted to die.

I silently but desperately pleaded, please don't make me do this.

The ferry docked at six in the evening and by seven we were on our way to Port Hamble.

As we passed a building on the corner, Marco stopped. The building had Universal Yachting written in big letters across the top.

'I just want to see if they can tell me where to start,' he said.

Chapter 6

Sunshine is Born

'They want to show us something tomorrow,' he said when he returned to the car, 'but it's a rear cockpit, so I don't know if it'll be any good. We may as well see it. We seem to be coming to a dead end.'

We had decided we needed a centre cockpit after seeing the Contest and the Westerly, both with very large double aft cabins. I imagined a pointed bed again.

'Hmmm,' I doubted, shaking my head.

We turned up at the agency at the appointed time. The owner was a UK distributor of power boats and had bought this sailboat 18 months earlier as a hobby. He had bought a bigger, faster sailboat to race at Cowes.

The morning was dismal and heavy, but that was nothing compared to my heart. They motored us out to the middle of the bay where the boat was moored. It was a 44-foot Gib'Sea Master, looking lonely, abandoned and wet. We climbed on board. It was now raining and cold. The sky was

The Year of Sunshine

black, and the sea a forbidding grey, and I wondered again how anyone in their right mind could enjoy sailing in England in this weather.

The boat was almost brand-new inside. The forward double master cabin was airy and spacious, the main saloon and galley area large and well-planned, and the two aft cabins roomy enough. I recognised the teak panelling from photographs in Marco's yachting magazines.

The agent showed us the electrical panel, the four batteries under the floorboards, the motor, which Marco made me climb down to look at, the extra sails, and all the things anyone knowing about boats would need to see. It all went over my head. I was anxious about being so close to the cold water outside.

'What did you think?' asked Marco, on the way back to the hotel.

'I didn't like it,' I said, resolutely.

'What didn't you like?' he shot back at me, incredulously.

'Everything.' I responded.

'Everything!' he exploded. 'It was beautiful, and has very good resale value.'

Aha. Did I detect a glimmer of hope for me? Perhaps he didn't intend to subject me to this torture for the rest of my life, only for this summer after all.

'It was too expensive, though,' he said. 'You must help me get the price down.'

'Me? But I don't even want the fucking thing!' I protested.

'Listen,' he tried to reason with me, 'you may as well resign yourself to the fact that I am committed to having a boat. I know you are waiting for me to change my mind, but

Sunshine is Born

I won't. We can continue looking—staying at cheap hotels and driving the entire summer which I know you hate, or you can help me get the price down on this one. Or you can go home, but I don't know why you would want to do that. I'm going to stay here. And the kids are arriving in twenty days. You'd be the better negotiator in this case, because you're English, it'll help us avoid any misunderstandings.'

He was probably right. He was not a patient man. His Latin temperament showed through and he hated long drawn-out deals which this could be since he did not want to pay the asking price.

I clenched my teeth and ran through my options. I didn't like any of them.

The sooner he got his boat, the sooner this seemingly endless searching would finish.

Francesca and her fiancé were arriving in a little under three weeks. The tickets had been booked way back in March, as soon as she had found out the vacation dates from her study courses. I couldn't wait to see them, I couldn't disappoint them and, perhaps, I would have an ally.

All right, I'd get him his boat. I could always go back with Francesca after her holiday.

I made a few phone calls including one to the agent. The agent was pleased I was interested, but doubted the owner would accept my offer.

We went out to look at the boat again. It was colder and raining harder, and I liked it even less than the first time.

Marco was getting quite excited about it.

We looked at other boats just in case this one didn't come off, but nothing compared.

The Year of Sunshine

'Why are they taking so long in deciding?' Marco was impatient to get started.

'Well, they want to sell it to us, and we want to buy it, it's just a question of arriving at a price agreeable to both parties.' I tried to placate him.

'It wouldn't take me that long to decide,' was his irritated response.

But, of course, he just had to wait it out.

The creaky hotel we were staying at was not great, so while we were waiting we decided to spend a couple of days at a hotel in the country. We asked around, and a number of people recommended a hotel on the moors at Burley.

I had never seen moors before, only heard about bodies of murdered girls found there when I was little. So it was with some misgivings, overcome by a need to relax and be pampered for a few days, that I agreed to go and have a look. The old hotel was set in lovely grounds, and after Marco had checked out the dining room and menu, we took a room for a week.

The weather was cold. Thunderclouds rumbled, threatening storms, and the north wind blew, freezing us as we walked over the moors, obliging us to draw our jackets closer around our bodies for warmth. One day, during a walk through a small copse, we heard a rustle and saw some movement in the trees to our left. I had a spooky feeling that we were being watched. We came to a clearing and saw our would-be attackers—a small group of ponies pulling leaves from the trees. There were groups of ponies all over the moors, amongst the briar bushes. It was a lovely sight to see the mares, with their foals close by their sides, running skittishly, or standing eating.

Sunshine is Born

The hotel was gracious with co-operative management. They let us change rooms twice because of the noise. This time it wasn't the traffic, but the milkman and garbage collector who came at five-thirty in the morning.

We had given the agent the hotel phone number, and Marco listened for every phone call. Finally, it came. I took it. The price was still too high. I offered them back their spinnaker sail—I didn't anticipate using it, I didn't even know what it was for. They would call back. They did and said OK—the spinnaker sail clinched the deal. I went back to Marco with the news. He could hardly contain himself.

His dream was coming true. For me, the nightmare was just beginning.

There was so much to be done. It was 4 June.

We left Burley that day and found a new hotel in Southampton.

We discussed at length how we were going to get the boat to the South of France, and where we would moor it. We had been warned many times that permanent moorings during the summer were impossible. You can get a few days here or there, but weeks, they said, forget it.

There was not enough time for us to sail the boat over in time for Francesca's arrival. Thank God, at least I was saved from that one.

'We can truck it over for you,' offered the agent. The previous owner, being in the boat business, kindly offered to arrange customs papers.

'But we don't know where to truck it,' I said, desperately.

'Don't worry about that.' he said. 'I'll have my agent in Golfe Juan find you a mooring for a month to get you

The Year of Sunshine

started, and you can find your own way from there.' I couldn't thank him enough. That was a big problem taken care of.

'Now, what are you going to call the boat and we'll get a new name put on for you.'

'Sunshine,' I said without thinking.

After I said it, I realised that we hadn't given a thought to a name before. I looked at Marco for approval. He nodded, smiling. He liked it, or perhaps he was just pleased that I had named the boat.

When I was little, and my father came home on leave from the war, he used to pick me up and sing me a song which always made me feel happy.

'You are my sunshine, my only sunshine, you make me happy when skies are grey.' Skies couldn't be much greyer for me than now. I felt so vulnerable.

'And I would like the letters yellow and fat and round and happy,' I said, confirming the desire to be comforted.

'No problem,' he said.

He made everything sound so easy.

'When's the soonest you can get it on a truck?' we asked.

'Well, we have a boat being delivered over the weekend, it can be loaded on that truck and leave on Monday morning.'

Good. It would take a week to organise everything. I also wanted to get bed linen in England; continental quilts and pillows were cheaper in the UK and you couldn't beat good old 'Marks and Sparks' quality.

I rushed about Southampton, collecting blankets and sheets, quilts, pillows and a typewriter, and put it all on board.

Sunshine is Born

Marco bought *How to* books—*How to navigate*, *How to cruise*, *How to use your boat's radio*, *How to do your own repairs*. He proudly showed me what he had bought.

'Now we have plenty of reading,' he said.

'But you told me we would take courses,' I responded desperately.

'There's no time now, is there,' he replied logically. 'It'll all make sense when we get on board, and if we have a problem, we'll get somebody to come and show us.'

My heart sank. I knew he wouldn't. He'd rather die in the attempt finding out for himself than ask for help.

Monday morning we were at the boatyard, bright and early, to watch the boat loaded on to the truck. When we got there it was already sitting out of the water on the boat lift with the mast off ready to be stored. I looked at the huge boat with its huge mast, and thought, Oh Christ, this is really happening. That's our boat up there. We're going to be sailing that boat.

Who would have thought a year ago that I'd be here now looking up at a sailboat I owned, but didn't want? I tried to trace the sequence of events up to now. The whole thing had been against my better judgement from the start. I had been manipulated and pressured into it. But with Marco's determination, it had almost taken on a life-force of its own.

'There's got to be a reason for all this, there's just got to be,' I told myself. I can't be going through all this for no reason. Though none of it made any sense to me yet.

It was a freezing day. Even the boathands and truck driver were commenting how cold it was even though it was early June.

The Year of Sunshine

The sign-writer finished painting our new name, and the boat looked happier already. It seemed to take forever to get it loaded on to the enormous truck. The truck was booked on the four o'clock ferry from Southampton. They finished with ten minutes to spare and Marco raced over to the terminal to ask them to hold the ferry. The truck wouldn't arrive in the south of France before Friday because trucks were only allowed on French roads at night in certain areas.

We said our thankyous and goodbyes, and hoped to catch the six o'clock ferry from Dover. We had to pick up a document for the car from London, but we figured two hours should do it. Unfortunately, we hadn't considered the peak-hour traffic and getting lost, so we didn't leave London until after six and only just made the last ferry. By the time we unloaded the car in Calais, it was getting on for eleven-thirty. We tried five or six hotels before we found a room available which we thought unusual for that time of the year. We found out later it was because our ferry had been the last one for 11 days because of a strike from midnight that night.

We drove through two days of torrential rain, storm, thunder and lightning. At one point we couldn't see the highway it was so bad, and we had to stop under a bridge because of hail. As we neared the Riviera, the sun broke through and by the time we arrived at Golfe Juan, the weather was beautiful.

And, thus started my love affair with Golfe Juan.

Although I have been to the French Riviera many times, I had never heard of this engaging little town so characteristic of the region.

It's off *Route Nationale* 7, RN7, and nestled between Juan-les-Pins and Cannes. It has one main road which leads

Sunshine is Born

down from the RN7 and a couple of small streets criss-crossing it.

It was not yet touristy like its neighbours and had a very 'small French village' atmosphere. There you will find the *boucherie* (butcher) who will give you the best meat for whatever you're making and cut it just the way you need it, and all done with a smile. He will even tell you how to cook it. Next, you will find a great *marchand de fruits et légumes* (fruit and vegetable shop) and it was here we discovered wild peaches. They are flat and look like a donut with a stone in the middle and they have the most spectacular taste. You will also find three or four *boulangerie-pâtisseries* for the baguettes and half a dozen other types of bread while you're at it, and of course, French pastries—enough said. It has a good *presse* (paper shop) where we bought our *Financial Times* every day, and *Time* magazine once a week. There are a few bars and restaurants, a couple of small supermarkets, a wonderful *fromagerie* for cheeses and fresh pastas, the best *institut de beauté*, a good *coiffeuse*, a *cardiologue* (heart specialist), which I had occasion to use once because I rode my bike too fast up a hill and nearly passed out. (He said I had the strongest heart he had ever examined, although sometimes I had doubts about this.) Plus a *pharmacie* and a few other little shops that one might have occasion to use, and *voilà* you had everything you could want.

And there were the roses, everywhere sold wonderful Nice roses. They came in hues ranging from yellow through coral to deep orange. The coral ones were my favourites. Most restaurants had bowls of them on the tables. They are spectacular.

The port was only recently finished, which explained why it still had moorings available. It was well-designed—new, pretty, clean, uncluttered, and very up-market. It had a row of elegant shops and restaurants lining the street side of the port. Restaurant tables spilled onto the promenade, their colourful tablecloths and umbrellas fluttering now and again in a slight sea breeze. The sea side of the port was lined by a flower garden where the big luxurious motor yachts were moored. They had names like *Princess*, *My Dream*, *Queen of my Heart* and other exotic names.

There was also a *théâtre de mer* (open-air theatre).

I couldn't believe our luck.

'Ooh darling, I like this,' I enthused.

'Good, I was afraid you wouldn't,' he commented sarcastically.

I'd deserved that. I had been a royal pain in the arse. We still had two days before the boat arrived on Friday morning. We familiarised ourselves with the area, rediscovered Cannes, Juan-les-Pins and Baie des Anges, much loved places from years ago, when Francesca was born in Nice.

Then, the big day. Marco was up at six to go down to the port. I luxuriated in bed, and then had a leisurely breakfast of croissants and *café au lait*.

It might be my last, I figured, I may as well enjoy it.

I ambled down to the port, past the pink villas with their colourful gardens and through the town. It was a beautiful morning, sun shining, not too hot. I tried to anticipate what was ahead of me but couldn't even hazard a guess.

I found Marco at the *chantier* (boatyard). The boat had been there since four in the morning and they already had it in the water and were preparing to fit the mast. I climbed aboard. It was filthy from travelling in the storms.

'Stay here in case the guy needs anything; I have to go to customs,' said Marco clutching a handful of papers.

I smiled nervously at the wiry youth struggling with the mast. I felt so helpless, so out of my element. I didn't know where to walk without falling over winches and deck hatches.

I decided to sit on the quay where I felt more secure. Jean-Paul (the young Frenchman putting on the mast) and I exchanged a few pleasantries, I got him something to drink, but otherwise I just sat and stared miserably at my future.

'Marco, I will never forgive you for this,' I numbly told myself.

After much struggling and mumbling, the mast was finally in place and secured.

'*C'est fini*,' a sweaty Jean-Paul told me.

I went to find Marco and we returned with the man who was going to motor the boat to its mooring for us.

'This is a big boat to manoeuvre,' he said, 'and it only has one screw, so you must see where it pulls to, forward right and reverse left, or vice versa.'

I had no idea what he was talking about so I closed my eyes and prayed I would never have to manoeuvre.

We got into position on the second or third try.

A shouted instruction brought me back from my reverie.

'Fenders! Boathook!'

I looked at the man at the wheel wondering what he was expecting me to do.

The Year of Sunshine

I spread my hands and shook my head, my eyebrows raised in question. I must have made a pathetic sight. I read his mind in that split second, 'Useless bloody woman!' Unreasonably, I instantly hated him. Fuck you! I thought, and fuck all men!

Marco didn't know what to do either, and he's not exactly Jack-Be-Nimble, but he showed a bit more enterprise than I did, and he and Jean-Paul managed to moor the boat adequately. I climbed gratefully on to the pontoon.

'OK,' said the man, 'she's all yours.'

It's hard to describe how I felt when I heard those words. I suppose nauseous with fear would be close.

There had been only one other time in my life when I had the same feeling—that my life was genuinely in danger. It was many years ago when we were very young. We had just arrived in Sao Paulo, Brazil, and were invited on a trip to the coast some nine hours away, the last part through the jungle. We were almost at the end of the journey when our car broke down. It was night time, raining and the jungle was dense and terrifying. We had been given a gun for protection, but it was when a group of drunken workers from a nearby camp approached the car that I feared for my life. Luckily our companion reappeared and we were able to proceed through the jungle to civilization.

I looked at our *Sunshine* and wondered how on earth we were going to manage. Ridiculously, even the thought of getting our enormous suitcases on board was going to be a challenge without a gangplank—it was a big jump across.

'We move in tomorrow,' said Marco. The finality was frightening.

Sunshine is Born

We had no idea about anything. Being thrown in the deep end without knowing how to swim would have to be an understatement.

'Well, what do we do now?' I asked as I climbed back on board.

The previous owner had told us that the electricity plug would certainly have to be changed when we got to the Continent, so that was number-one job. Jean-Paul changed this for us. Number-two job was to fill the water tanks if they needed filling. We looked at the instruments on the electricity panel which said 'Tanks—Full or Empty', and the arrow pointed to Full, although this seemed strange, since we thought the previous owner would have emptied the tanks for the road trip, but we just assumed he had forgotten or not considered it necessary.

We sat at the dining room table. I wanted to be anywhere but here. Impending doom was all that was on my mind.

I was very nervous. I needed to go to the bathroom.

'How do you flush the water?' I asked.

'I don't know,' said Marco. 'You have to do something with a valve and then pump, I seem to remember the agent said.'

I turned the tap on. No water came out.

'How do I get water?'

'Don't ask me, read the instruction books,' was his reply.

I went into one of the aft cabins, sat down, picked up one of the *How to* books Marco had piled in there, and burst into tears. I hated this with a purple passion.

Was I going to have to read the instructions for every step I took on this blasted boat?

The Year of Sunshine

Marco poked his head around the door. When he saw the floods of tears, he took me in his arms.

I think he was beginning to feel as helpless as I did.

'Look, it will take us a bit of time to get to know the boat. We'll just take it day by day, and if we really hate it that much, we'll sell it, all right?'

'Promise?' I asked sulkily through my tears.

'Promise.'

'All right,' I agreed miserably.

'Now we must go and get all the stuff we need to clean the boat with, and make it as much like home as possible.'

At which point, I burst into tears again.

On one of our exploratory drives before the boat arrived, we had discovered a place just behind Antibes called Sophia Antipolis. It had a gigantic supermarket called Carrefour and several huge shopping outlets. We spent the afternoon collecting the cleaning materials we needed to scrub and whiten the boat, and polish the wooden panelling. We chose everything we would need to make the boat like home and selected a small microwave oven, electric hotplates—I wasn't used to gas—a vacuum cleaner, a television, a totally impractical but beautiful coffee machine (which had to be wrapped in towels every time we moved the boat in case it fell and smashed), an iron (which I used once only), a toaster, an electric mixer (which I never used), and what seemed like 30 bags of food. Canned goods and mineral water took up most of this. If I had felt unsafe before, now I was convinced the boat would sink under the weight of all these cans and bottles.

By the time we had finished it was too late for much else, so we returned to the hotel for our last night on land.

Sunshine is Born

The next morning we set to work cleaning the boat. We scrubbed and scrubbed. It was filthy. By midday it was hot, and we were exhausted from hosing and scrubbing but we kept going. The next step was the whitening liquid, which we rubbed in and hosed off. The boat was starting to look new again.

Pleased with our efforts but needing a break, we walked over and bought ice-creams from a new bar, near where we had parked our car, and just in front of the port. The owners had opened two weeks previously. They were so sweet, both young in their middle twenties. They had seen our comings and goings, as we passed them every time we unloaded the car. They couldn't believe so much stuff going on a sailboat. Normally people go on board with a duffle bag each, and maybe a box of food and drinks, but for us, it had been like moving house.

We chatted with them and told them we were new to the game (as if they hadn't guessed). They were very kind and tried to help with anything they could. They even sent an English skipper over to the boat to give us a few pointers. He explained the instruments to us, and how to use the electrical panel, and turn on the water pressure and use the bilge pump.

So far, so good.

I made up the beds, and was pleased with my choice of pale blue for the sheets and quilts.

We had a makeshift dinner that night, since the hotplates had not been delivered yet and we didn't know how to use the gas stove—there didn't appear to be any gas connected and I didn't yet know about the safety valve. We had walked

The Year of Sunshine

into town and bought baguettes, *rillette* (a delicious coarse pâté made with pork and lard), a couple of packets of grated heart of celery and carrots, some cakes and a bottle of local wine. The previous owner of the boat had kindly donated a full set of very nice cutlery and plates as a gift, so we were set up.

I was very conscious of the water below me and around me, and it made me feel very uncomfortable to be separated from it by only a thin fibreglass hull. And there were noises that I didn't understand. Every now and then, something beeped, sometimes more than others, and it took us a couple of days to realise that it came from the battery charger. I wanted to ask Marco whether that was good or bad, but I knew he wouldn't know and probably wouldn't care.

He was having a great time, and gleefully showed me every little discovery he made.

'Angel, come and look at this,' he would call excitedly, as I tried to find ingenious places for all our clothes and belongings, shaking my head in despair at the little space available.

'Angel, come here and help me.'

'See how this works. Isn't that great?'

At least one of us was having a good time.

As it got darker we turned the interior boat lights on. We thought they would be very dim, but they turned out to be quite good when connected to onshore electricity. We hadn't bargained on the mosquitoes though, and made Mozzie-Zappers the next day's number-one priority.

We went to bed early because we were so tired. The bed was a strange shape. Although large, it had a narrower end, following the shape of the boat, though it didn't come to a

Sunshine is Born

point like some I had seen (there was a locker between us and the bow). We put the pillows there, and they just fitted, squashed up close together. We found it quite cramped that way and I wondered how I would put up with Marco's snoring right in my ear. Since the bottom of the bed was like a regular double bed we discussed whether we should put the pillows at that end, but then the pillows fell off because there was nothing to stop them, so we remade the bed the way it had been.

In that particular cabin, which was very spacious, there were three large deck hatches, two portholes and another large deck hatch in the ensuite bathroom making six openings in all. Marco, being a fresh-air fanatic, insisted on having every one of these wide open. I, on the other hand, prefer a warm bedroom (I travel with my own electric blanket in winter), but I made no comment this evening, just to show a willingness to try to co-operate at least. But I couldn't sleep anyway because of the rocking of the boat and the strange noises, which are amplified inside a boat. There was a noise like static electricity; the noise of the fenders squeaking each time they rubbed up against the next boat; and a metal-on-metal noise we couldn't identify for weeks. We found out later that this was a loose halyard hitting against the mast in the wind. Then there was the wind in the masts, which sounded like ghosts sighing, together with the clicking of the halyards on the other boats, it all made a weird orchestration.

So out came the sleeping pills again.

The worst thing for me was waking up at four o'clock in the morning, covered with dew. It was like taking a cold

The Year of Sunshine

shower while I was asleep, then waking up freezing and wet. I grabbed my pillows and crept down to one of the back cabins, shut the portholes and deck hatch, closed the door, and snuggled underneath the continental quilt, and slept there for the rest of the night, and much of the summer. (The freedom of having another cabin to retire to was very convenient, as it meant that I could read until after midnight if I felt like it, and not be disturbed by Marco's snoring.)

Next morning for breakfast, we had coffee from our new coffee machine, which worked quite well, and cereals with milk. The fridge was also very strange. Unlike kitchen fridges with shelves, this fridge or I should say these fridges, since there were two, were deep, and you had to load things on top of one another, which was so impractical. And particularly impractical for me because, being small, I couldn't even reach the bottom of the fridge. I had to continually unload the fridge completely because I always needed something at the very bottom, or something that had slipped to the very bottom. I also had to devise a way to keep the cover (door) open, otherwise it would slam down on your head while you were fishing around inside. The milk and the drinks, which were usually in plastic bottles or containers, would fall over unless you secured them. We later discovered we could avoid this by putting the yoghurts and small items in big boxes and transferring the milk into glass juice bottles with screw caps and wedging them between the bigger boxes. It took us a few days to work this all out, and the first few days were quite disastrous, with milk and soft drinks spilling inside the fridge.

I couldn't have felt more out of place if I had landed on Mars.

Sunshine is Born

After breakfast we continued cleaning and organising. We had done quite a bit the day before, but there was still a lot to be done. The sails also had to be put on. Jean-Michel, a friend of Jean-Paul, came and helped Marco install the sail, then the jib. I kept looking at that huge mainsail and jib, and thinking, my God, am I ever going to be able to handle this when we are on our own? To me, it was very, very scary.

Marco loved every minute of it. This was a whole new world to be discovered, and he thrived on it.

So the day wore on, and early in the afternoon, after Jean-Michel had left, a new sound started. It was a high-pitched whirring sound. I panicked. I was sure we had done something, or hadn't done something, and the boat was ready to blow out of the water. We didn't know what to do, we didn't know how to stop it—we didn't even know what it was. And this whole thing with the electricity and water didn't sit comfortably with me either.

We had noticed that the boat moored next to us had an Italian flag, and some people had come on board Friday night. We had said '*Ciao*' and '*Buona sera*' to them, but that was all.

I begged Marco, '*Please* go and ask the people next door what this noise can be.'

He returned with a young Italian fellow, Roberto, who identified the noise as the water pressure pump, saying that the water tanks must be empty. He turned the water pressure off at the panel. Thank God the noise stopped.

But it can't be that, we said to him, look, the instruments show the tanks are full.

'Oh don't take any notice of that,' he said, 'the instruments hardly ever work on boats. They always go wrong.'

The Year of Sunshine

This was not good news. I had been relying on the instruments at least being accurate and telling me what I needed to know, and here was the first proof that they weren't going to be working half of the time. This was another blow for me.

He asked us how to fill the tanks.

Well, all we knew was that there was a water inlet up on deck, where we had to insert the hose, but we had no idea about anything else, like changing tanks over or anything. It was a complete mystery to us.

'Well, you must know,' said Roberto, 'you must find out all of these things because it's very important.' And he spent a good hour or two lifting up the floorboards, tracing all the plumbing, and showing us that there was a change-over switch from one tank to the other. We looked at these two enormous tanks underneath our floorboards and saw instruments on them too, but which obviously didn't work since they were showing full as well.

'You must know everything about your boat,' he said, 'because every boat is different.' He explained to us that he had been a skipper for several years, and they (he and his wife) chartered boats, and every time he practically took the boat apart to find out how everything worked, so that he knew what was going on. This wasn't something I wanted to have to do, but obviously we had to do it.

So we unravelled the mystery of the water tanks and water pressure, and we started filling the tanks. The noise from those tanks filling was enough to give me heart failure. The air would explode with a resounding booommm, just when you least expected it, and it sounded as though another boat had hit us. It was a shock until you got used to it. More

Sunshine is Born

noises to get used to. Anyway, we were pleased we had solved that problem.

We asked Roberto how we knew when the tanks were full, and he showed us a little overflow outlet on the hull just below the water inlet. It took me months to realise that there was a corresponding one on the other side which, instead of flowing down the side of the boat, coughed and spluttered up into the air. I never knew what it was until I finally got curious enough to investigate and found that it was turned the wrong way, pointing up into the air instead of down towards the water, obviously displaced during transportation.

That whole week, we were scurrying around like a pair of squirrels preparing for winter, in readiness for Francesca and Luke's arrival on Saturday, six days away. We had to find practical places for everything and install the new appliances, bearing in mind that everything had to be belted or screwed down for when we cruised, and in such an unfamiliar environment, it wasn't easy. Jean-Michel shook his head in bewilderment when we showed him all the things and I think he looked upon every item as a new challenge and took a certain pride in solving the problem.

The microwave had to have rings and belts fitted to secure it, and the TV needed a wall support since we had bought a television larger than the average boat has so there was no really practical place for it. It also had to be belted and secured somewhere when we sailed, and we created a place for it on the coffee table by drilling holes in the large wooden pedestal base, and threading strong belts through, up and over, which worked well. The wall bracket was hard to find, and we had half the port searching for one for us.

The Year of Sunshine

Through the grapevine the residents of the port had found out we were complete novices and everybody offered to help. We had a constant flow of visitors. Jim, the English skipper, was an ex-singer and pub-owner who liked to unwind by skippering other people's boats. David and his girlfriend were Aussies, also skippering on the Riviera (David uncannily turned up in a T-shirt which had the word 'sunshine' splashed across the front). The couple from the bar, the brother of the girl from the bar, and his friend all came to see if they could help. Jean-Michel, friend of Jean-Paul, came every lunchtime to help us install our appliances, and installed the Loran C, (a navigational instrument) which our Italian neighbour taught me how to use. We were a bit of a curiosity, to say the least, and a source of great amusement. A couple of mad middle-aged Aussies is how they saw us, I'm sure.

But they weren't critical, they enjoyed helping. There is a camaraderie in the boat world which I have never come across anywhere else.

We would rush back and forth on our little bikes to the *chantier* for screws, rings, and cords, or the supermarket for something else we had forgotten, or into the little town of Golfe Juan for our breakfast croissants and lunchtime baguettes.

The midday sun was becoming a problem. It was very hot, and there was no escape from the heat. On deck you fried, in the cabin you roasted. I have never sweated so much in my life, my head sweated and the perspiration ran down my forehead and neck.

I now understood why people on boats don't iron their clothes. It was a total waste of time in that heat and humidity.

Sunshine is Born

As soon as you put anything on, it became crumpled. And so, even I learned to wear un-ironed T-shirts and shorts. I was progressing. Gone was the elegant chignon, my long hair was now worn in a ponytail. Most of the time I was dressed in a swimming costume or bikini, even the long red nails were gone now, and I was acquiring a deep tan. And I was re-acquiring a long forgotten persona. There were some aspects of this kind of life that appealed. I knew I was adapting physically, but mentally there was still a lot of work to be done.

Marco was pleased with my transformation.

'You're beginning to look like you again,' he said admiringly, hugging me.

'Are you happy about it?' I asked, flirting with him.

'Yes, but you are not completely with me yet, are you?' This immediately dampened the spirit of the moment.

He knew of the turmoil that was going on in my mind. I had, perhaps stupidly, voiced my intention of going back with Francesca if, at the end of her stay, it hadn't worked out. He knew that half of me was with him and half was in Sydney. I could understand that he needed to do this, he wanted to move on from the restrictions of running a business, and get back to nature, but I did not feel the need to.

He was so enjoying his freedom again. He had stopped smoking just before we left—he'd been up to two packs a day—and was putting on a little weight from all the good eating. At the office, he never had time to eat but was always accompanied by a cup of black coffee, which would sit next to his computer, together with a lit cigarette.

He, too, was getting deeply tanned. He was letting his hair and beard grow and looked carelessly rugged. His outward appearance belied his mental state. He cared very much that I was on knife's edge. He knew he could either lose me or find me, and it did not make for a relaxed state of mind. Consequently, arguments would erupt over nothing. Sometimes they would blow over; sometimes they would blow up.

And the heat didn't help. By nature, Marco was hot-blooded and fiery, and the added assault by the Mediterranean sun encouraged his argumentative nature, of which I was a defiant recipient.

It took little to elicit an angry response from me. I was still reluctant about this whole thing but desperately wanted to mend our relationship. I was there for that, not for the boat. Sometimes we were loving and tender, and I thought we were making progress, but then something would need to be done with the boat and sparks would fly. When we were loving I was encouraged, when we were fighting I doubted whether we would ever be able to make the relationship work again. But I was going to persevere through the whole summer, determined to see it right to the end, whatever the end brought.

We had to do something about the heat in the boat. We searched all over for an awning, one that covered most of the boat. A custom-made one would cost us 8,000 French francs which we weren't prepared to pay, but a thorough investigation of the market turned up a ready-made light one for half the price. It took us ages to work out how to install it. It needed a wooden bar inserted at the cockpit end to hold it out from where it was clipped to the backstay. We bought a thick wooden curtain rod the entire width of the sunshade for this purpose, and couldn't understand why it

Sunshine is Born

kept wobbling down on one side and up on the other and vice versa in the slightest breeze. After a couple of days of studying how other ones were installed (and they are all different), we realised that the pole had to be much shorter, matching the width at the back of the cockpit, and then held down with cords clipped to the metal guard rails.

This contraption turned out to be one of our best buys—it not only cooled down the boat inside, provided shade on deck, but also avoided that awful humidity that came down during the night.

The gangplank was the last thing we needed, and it was installed on the Friday. Hallelujah, we could finally walk across, which was certainly more civilised than jumping.

The boat was finally ready. She looked beautiful, sparkling white with a new royal blue mainsail hood, and *Sunshine* proudly displayed in the fat, happy, yellow letters on the stern. She looked as though she belonged to the Riviera, with its hot blue sky, brilliant sunshine, and shimmering turquoise water.

Inside the boat smelled sweetly of polished wood panelling and the yellow roses, which I had placed in the centre of the large square teak dining table. The grey-blue upholstery blended beautifully with the pale blue of the sheets and matching blankets in the cabins, which could be glimpsed through the half-open doors, and a bowl of wild peaches and fresh figs decorated the small teak coffee table in the main saloon.

'*Vous avez un beau bateau, Madame.*' The awning maker had told me when he came to give me a quote.

I smiled in acknowledgement, but it was a bittersweet victory.

Chapter 7

A Temporary Truce is Declared

On Saturday morning Francesca and Luke were arriving. I was very excited as we drove down to Nice Airport to wait for them. It was the end of June, winter in Australia, and they arrived looking tired and pale from their 26-hour flight, but they perked up visibly as we walked out of the airport into the hot sunshine and landscaped car park, full of colourful Mediterranean flowers, and they got their first feel of the Riviera.

They were ecstatic about the car and extracted a promise from Marco to let them drive it at the first opportunity.

'My God, everything's so beautiful,' they repeated as we whisked them past St Laurent du Var, Antibes, Juan-les-Pins, finally arriving at my darling little Golfe Juan and the port.

The Year of Sunshine

Francesca fell instantly in love with the yacht. (I had not taken into consideration the fact that for a 19-year old, a yacht on the Mediterranean would be the last word in glamour, excitement and adventure—she was a lot like her father.)

If she was an ally, who needed enemies.

At the first opportunity when we were alone, Francesca asked me how it was going with Marco.

'Oh not too bad,' I replied, but she knew there was more.

'Daddy seems to be happy.'

'Yes, he is, he needed to do this, but I didn't. I don't know where it is all going to end yet.'

'Don't think about that part, just enjoy what you are doing now. You might find out that you did need to do it.' Wise words for one so young, but easier said that done.

And as if to prove she was truly Marco's daughter, within a day, she and Luke had explored the little town, the neighbouring beaches, and made friends with the bar owners. They'd also made friends with the owners of the *Bella Cherie*, the Italian sailboat moored next to us. Roberto, the young man we had met the first weekend, was a friend of the owner.

'Are we going out today?' Francesca had asked over breakfast the next morning.

I shot an alarmed glance at Marco.

'Why not?' he replied.

'We are not going out on our own,' I said adamantly.

'Why not?' Came the chorus.

Oh Christ.

I think I must have looked sick, because Marco agreed to ask Fabio, one of the owners of the *Bella Cherie*, if he would

A Temporary Truce is Declared

come out with us for the first time. Francesca had found out that he, like Roberto, was a sailing instructor.

He good-naturedly agreed. He came on board, looked around and could not believe what Marco had undertaken.

'*Ma sei matto?*' (Are you crazy?) he asked, truly impressed.

'*Ma ci vuole un bel coraggio!*' (You're pretty courageous!)

But Marco saw none of this.

'What's so difficult about sailing a boat?' He wanted to know.

'Plenty,' replied Fabio, 'You'll find out.'

I was on Fabio's side. But I knew he also had a sneaking admiration for Marco.

'OK, we'll go to Isles des Lérins. I'll bring my family too. It's a favourite place for the boats, between two islands. It's just opposite Cannes. The water is crystal clear and you can swim and fish. It's wonderful. We'll have lunch there. I'll ask Anna to prepare some things.'

Francesca, Luke and I walked quickly into town to pick up some fresh baguettes and ham. Silvana, Fabio's 10-year-old daughter, skipped along beside us.

'Is it true?' she asked.

'Is what true, darling?'

'That you've never been out on a sailboat before,' she said gleefully, sensing an exciting afternoon.

The little devil, even she was conspiring against me.

'Yes, it's true,' I replied miserably.

When we got back, the gangplank was off, sitting on the pontoon, the motor was ticking over, and Fabio was undoing the anchor rope.

My heart was in my mouth as I jumped across. I said a

silent prayer to my guardian angel, and asked not to be abandoned in this time of need.

Fabio and Marco manoeuvred the boat out of its narrow mooring. This was relatively easy because the bow was already pointing into the canal. Manoeuvring it back was going to be difficult because it had to backed in. We just missed the anchor chains of the other boats, and got into the main canal. Having four extra people on board to help push our boat off the fenders of the other boats and chains had made it light work. I was anticipating how I was going to be running from side to side when I was the only crew after Francesca and Luke left.

We got into open sea, and although it was a gloriously sunny day, the sea was a little choppy.

'Let's get the mainsail up then,' said Fabio. He and his wife worked as a team. I wondered if I would ever master the art of sailing. All those ropes. Where did they all lead and what did they all do?

They started explaining what they were doing, in Italian, of course. I speak Italian but I didn't know these new words, new names for everything. (By the end of the journey, I only knew the Italian names for the parts of the boat and the sheets and halyards.)

Marco was saying, 'Uh-huh,' nodding in understanding, although I knew he would have forgotten by the next day.

'Do you understand, Angel?' he kept asking me.

I was in no mood to be called 'angel', that was for sure, and I didn't want to understand. At the first big wave I disappeared below, holding on for dear life while the radio shot from one end of the shelf to the other, and all sorts of loose

A Temporary Truce is Declared

things fell around me. Luckily, they had secured the TV, microwave and coffee machine. Water was splashing in through a deck hatch I had left open (what did I know?) and the sea level was visible through the portholes—two-thirds of the way up. I grabbed the HRT tablets that I take daily, shoved the bottle down my costume front, made a mental note of where I had put my passport in case we went down, and released a tirade of fury against Marco, destiny, the world and anything else that got in the way.

I grasped the galley counter in an effort to keep myself upright, and turned on the tap to get some water intending to stick my head under to cool myself off, and it came out at an angle. That's all I bloody needed—crooked water! Hot angry tears flowed down my face. 'I'm leaving. I'm leaving,' I sobbed.

'Where's Angel?' I could hear Marco calling.

He was happy and excited and wanted to share this glorious moment of our maiden voyage with me.

Go drown yourself, I wanted to shout back, but we had guests and it took all I had to restrain myself from doing so.

I could hear Francesca shouting in excitement from the front, where she and Luke had stationed themselves in order to gain maximum effect of the hull hitting the waves, getting covered with spray. The flowers slid across the table and I just caught them in time.

Something else fell down with a loud clatter, and the doors banged (we later had hooks installed to keep them open), my bag fell to the floor and spilled its contents everywhere. I could hear everything shifting around in the fridge, and vaguely wondered what kind of omelette I would find at the bottom.

The Year of Sunshine

Oh Jesus, I hated this with every ounce of my being.

Francesca came laughing down the stairs to see where I was and was thrown on top of me as we hit another wave, and we landed in a tangled heap of legs and arms on a divan. We tried to get up but were thrown to the other side as the boat lurched again. She was hysterical with laughter by this time and she grabbed a rope which had been poked through a cockpit porthole, to steady herself, but instead of regaining her balance, she swung around it with the movement of the boat, and it ended up round her neck. It was very funny indeed. She was laughing so hard now she had to hang on for dear life, slipping and falling, and when she caught sight of the bottle down my costume front (she knew what it was as I'd always said the tablets would be the first thing I'd grab in an emergency), she collapsed on the floor, helpless with mirth. Seeing her there broke my enraged fury, and I clung on to the navigator's desk barely able to steady myself I was laughing so hard now.

We went back up on deck, and were nearly at the islands, thank goodness. A beautiful sight met my eyes. Moored on an expanse of crystal clear turquoise water, between two islands, were perhaps 20 or 30 sailboats and motor yachts of all sizes. Drenched with sun they lay there, their occupants quietly lunching, drinking, sunbathing, reading, and peacefully enjoying the glorious French Riviera.

Everyone went for a swim while I prepared lunch. It was so splendid, so peaceful that even I enjoyed it. It would have been churlish not to.

How could everything be so beautiful and yet not inspire only the most exquisite thoughts, I asked myself? Attitude, it's all in the attitude.

A Temporary Truce is Declared

We stayed there until about six in the evening, when it seemed as though a prearranged signal had been set off, and everybody started heading for home and showers to get ready to go out for dinner or eat in, whichever was the case.

Perhaps peak hour would have been a more appropriate description.

We pulled up our anchor and had to manoeuvre around a couple of big boats near us. I took the helm and was surprised how easy it was. Back at the port, Marco and Fabio motored the big boat down the main canal, into our narrow mooring canal and backed into our spot between the *Bella Cherie* and a 12-metre motor yacht.

'Bravo,' cried Fabio, as Marco went straight in first go. Anna jumped across to the pontoon, passed the ropes through the rings and threw them back to Fabio, who showed me how to secure them over the cleats. We arranged the fenders properly, and made sure we weren't touching the other boats.

Then started the ritual of hosing down the boat, showering, filling the tanks and preparing dinner. Francesca and Luke hosed themselves down on the quay as did most of the young people on the boats, and Marco used the proper shower in the bathroom while I made some coffee. Then I went in to shower. The noise from the bilge pump took a bit of getting used to, and being quite unfamiliar with the whole thing I didn't really know what to expect, except that while I was showering, the water in the shower recess was getting higher and higher, even though I had the bilge pump on.

I called out to Marco to check the outlet at the rear of the boat.

The Year of Sunshine

'Nothing's coming out,' he shouted.

Great! Hair lathered with shampoo, and dripping suds, I turned off the shower. I cursed this bloody boat for the umpteenth time and had to enlist Fabio's help again.

'You've got a blocked bilge pump,' he said. 'We must find the blockage and unblock it. Let's hope it's not the motor itself, or we might have a problem.'

So up came the floorboards, and we traced the hoses from the shower down the length of the boat through to the motor under the sink. Luckily the hoses were quite transparent, and it wasn't long before we discovered a dark blockage about a foot from the motor. We tried all sorts of things to unblock it. We tried blowing and sucking with a hand-pump, resulting in a broken pump. We pushed and we pulled, but the thing wouldn't budge.

'There's nothing for it,' said Fabio, 'you're going to have to cut it out and replace the piece of tubing.'

'FUCK,' I said, with great feeling. I had already had enough of this boat to last me a lifetime.

Fabio knew a few words of English and this was one of them. He laughed at me.

'Kid, you ain't seen nothin' yet.' Small consolation.

We cut into the tube and water gushed everywhere, overflowing the small bucket we had wedged into the small space, and out with it came the piece of plastic that had blocked the pipe. We were very fortunate that Luke could fix it, and the next day he was able to insert a new piece of tube into the cut piece. Every day we were learning something new about this boat the hard way.

Anna invited us to dinner. She made wonderful *spaghetti*

A Temporary Truce is Declared

pommarola with lots of garlic, and she showed me how to make a simple version of *pollo al vino con olive nere*. It's such an easy and quick thing to make—salt and pepper the pieces of chicken and fry with garlic until golden, add a glass of white wine and when absorbed add a handful of black olives and leave another five minutes—*e ecco pronto*!

The men walked into town and bought pastries and wine, and this set a pattern for most of our weekends in Golfe Juan.

We had an unexpected guest at dinner—the pale blue-eyed husky that guarded the boat about six down from us, hearing all the commotion, came up to investigate. Fabio, a dog lover, immediately got up and gave the dog a bowl of milk. From then on, at the same time every day, the husky would arrive at the gangplank without coming over, and sit and wait for his milk. He would take nothing else, and obediently Marco would get up and feed him.

Fabio was in and out of our boat a lot of the time. He was always showing Marco something or other.

On one occasion when he and I were in the saloon alone, he asked me how I was feeling about the boat, aware of my reluctance.

I shrugged.

'Marco took a big risk doing what he did,' he said.

'I know. But what can I do? I don't like it much, but I have to see this summer out.'

'*Poverina*,' he said sympathetically. 'Try not to worry too much, we'll be around most weekends and we'll teach you as much as we can.' He was a sweet man and the fact that he was there a lot of the time certainly helped me overcome my fears.

The Year of Sunshine

Weekends were always fun. There were six partners in Fabio's boat, so there were always two to six on board, plus invited friends, and many was the time we had nine or ten around our table, drinking wine and eating pasta, laughing and joking about our lack of expertise. They taught us a lot, those wonderful, fun-loving Italians, about life and about ourselves. They thought we were hilarious—Marco's conviction that nothing was impossible and my overwhelming fear that everything was difficult; Marco's determination to overcome everything and my determination not to.

We spent the following days showing Francesca and Luke around Cannes, where the film festival is held, and La Croisette with all the cafes frequented by the beautiful starlets and stars-to-be. It is really very glamorous. We showed them picturesque Antibes with its ancient city walls, and old fort, which is lit up at night, giving the port a romantic, dreamlike quality. We showed them Cros de Cagnes where Francesca was born and, at her insistence, even the clinic and nursery. We showed them Renoir's beautiful villa and garden at Cagnes. We showed them Monte Carlo, the palace and the Casino, and where the Formula One Grand Prix is held in the streets of Monaco. Every day, we walked into Golfe Juan to buy provisions for the boat, soaking up the atmosphere, stopping at the sidewalk cafes for *une noisette* (espresso with a dash of milk) or *une glace aux pistaches* (pistachio ice-cream), and we went swimming at the nearby beach. In the evenings, we would take long walks around the marina or along the promenade at Juan-les-Pins, buy a *crêpe Grand Marnier* from the kiosk and stand on the sidewalk eating it, along with the rest of the crowd.

A Temporary Truce is Declared

Everywhere was alive with excitement, gorgeous with flowers, and with an almost tangible air of expectancy. Holiday-makers were thronging in. The season had started. Sidewalk cafes, with live entertainment, were packed. Music from half a dozen places filled the air, waiters rushed around serving their specialties. The crowds were overflowing onto the roads, and it was becoming difficult to drive the car through the streets. It was alive. It was beautiful. It was magic.

Everyone had come to have a good time, they were dressed in true Riviera fashion—anything goes as long as it was eye-catching, pretty, different, outrageous.

Even the weather put on a special show. Although the weather is always good on the Riviera, this year it was fabulous, with temperatures climbing steadily and no hint of rain. We spent a day in Alassio, and Francesca and Luke outfitted themselves from head to toe. They were having a wonderful time and were already tanned from just a few days in the sun.

The following weekend we had Fabio's friends sleep on board because their boat was full. I had lost my voice and had a touch of bronchitis, so they all went out on Fabio's boat and left me to enjoy the peace and quiet, and rocking of the boat, on my own. I had actually started sleeping like a log. A lifetime light sleeper, I was agreeably surprised how the heat and the rocking of the boat lulled me off to sleep in an instant, and mosquitoes didn't disturb us at night because of the Mozzie-Zapper. We managed to keep them at bay at dusk with glass and brass lamps filled with coloured, perfumed insect-repellent oil that we lit every evening at dinner—they looked romantic and were very effective.

The Year of Sunshine

I was learning to sleep and live on board, but I couldn't cope yet with the sailing.

Marco and I had put off our differences while Francesca and Luke were there. We were enjoying their company so much that we didn't really have time to air our grievances. It was actually good for me, because Francesca's enjoyment of the boat really helped me too.

We had decided to show them Italy for five days so we left Golfe Juan at ten one morning and took the scenic A8 *autoroute* to Italy and were in Santa Margherita di Ligure in time for lunch. We went straight to *Da Alfredo*, settled ourselves at one of the tables on the pavement under the awning and, again, had our favourite meal there—*antipasto di mare*, *spaghetti al cartoccio* and plenty of Chianti. We sat there in the heat, finishing our coffees and watching the world go by: the noisy, sun-tanned Italians; the impatient, slow-moving cars; the sailboats which moved lazily in the bay as small waves gently lapped the beach; the sun creating tiny sparkling diamonds on the water; and we savoured every single moment.

We made our way to Monte Magno, in the hills of Tuscany where we had booked a hotel we had come across in Viareggio a couple of months back. This hotel was well-known for its wonderful cuisine—Tuscan cooking is amongst the best in the world, in my opinion—and the owners were so friendly.

It is set in the most beautiful countryside, and is fresh and cool because it is in the hills. In the morning there is a crispness in the air, and it smells of earth, wet leaves, wood fires and cappuccino. After dark, the fireflies look like fairy lights in the black night.

A Temporary Truce is Declared

It is inspiration for poets, writers and painters. There is a oneness with basic instincts, it is rich and profound. And there is true passion in the air.

The excitement over the World Cup was building to a crescendo. The matches were always in the evening, and everyone in the restaurants and bars sat transfixed by the TV sets. Where there was no TV in the restaurant, there was always one in the bar, and every time the shout 'goal' went up everyone ran to the TV to watch the replay and speculate on the score and the result. The first time it happened we couldn't believe our eyes. A shout went up and the restaurant emptied except for us. We looked around, surprised, wondering where everybody was running to. Not being a football enthusiast, Marco thought there was a fire. We decided we had better see what it was all about, and from that moment on, I too, became a World Cup follower. It was wonderfully exciting, and Luke and I ran with the crowd at every mealtime game.

On semi-final night, parties and gatherings were organised everywhere. The Italians wanted so badly to win. Had they won, I think there would have been celebrations all year long. It was a great evening. We all got settled in the bar lounge. Excitement was nearing fever pitch. A few arguments broke out, and tempers flared, mostly over Maradona playing for Argentina.

They watched with bated breath as the game was played, the usual jeers, shouts and comments going on as the game drew to a close. It was a one-all draw. Extra time was played, but still no result, so the penalty shoot-out began. One goal each, two goals each, the suspense was too much. One or two walked

The Year of Sunshine

out unable to bear it. Three goals each, then the Italian player missed and Argentina kicked the winning goal. The disappointment was tangible. You could feel their hearts breaking, their anger at being betrayed, at losing their beloved game. They walked off in disgust, each one silently mourning. It was a quiet night. You could feel their stunned disbelief at losing.

Next day in the bar for breakfast, the post-mortems began. The more intelligent ones calmed the angry ones saying, it's only a game. But they weren't to be placated, their first love had betrayed them, they weren't going to quieten down so easily. And so it went on for a couple of days, but after that, nothing more was mentioned. The affair was over. Passion and fire had been spent. They would find another topic to argue about.

We spent beautiful days in the hills of Tuscany, visiting the marble mountains of Carrara, watching huge pieces of marble cut, to be transported down to the valley, and then on to adorn bathrooms and foyers and facades all over the world. Marvellous colours could be seen in the excavations, ranging from blacks, greys, burgundies, pinks, many hues of beige through to marbled white then to the perfectly pure white used by sculptors. Michelangelo used this white marble for his works, including David and La Pietà. The mountains are really quite exceptional in that they appear to be permanently covered with snow. In reality, the whiteness comes from the effect of the marble quarries. There are some 300 quarries still operating today.

The little town at the very top, called Colonata, is ancient with a town square surrounded by taverns outside of which the old people sit watching the world go by. While we were

A Temporary Truce is Declared

parked, sitting half in and half out of our car, eating wonderful *prosciutto crudo* sandwiches from the deli, the local kids were playing football. They must have been aged from eight to twelve. The ball was kicked in our direction, and I playfully growled, 'Watch it'. The referee came over to me and miserably shook his head. *'Ma, non capiscono niente. Non sanno giocare.'* (I'm sorry. They don't understand a thing. They have no idea how to play.) The funny thing was this wise old man would have been all of ten years old.

We went to Lucca for the day. We love Lucca, where Marco was born. Puccini was also born here. It's a fascinating place, dating back beyond the times of Julius Caesar. Its architecture is magnificent, ranging from the severe Roman to the most sumptuous Renaissance, resulting in unsurpassed harmony. The superb churches of San Michele and San Martino integrate splendidly with the noble palaces built four or five hundred years later. The Roman amphitheatre, the tiny squares and water fountains, and ever-present ringing of church bells contribute to its wonderful air of history. Lucca is one of the last remaining places with an intact wall surrounding the city. It is said that there are 101 churches in one square mile, and one of its tallest towers has a much-photographed tree growing out of the top.

It was here that, as a little boy, Marco had returned home one winter day without his coat. His mother had asked him where it was.

'It's on the angel,' the little boy had replied.

'Which angel?' his mother wanted to know.

'The one in the piazza, Mammina. The little angel was cold so I gave her my coat,' he had explained.

The Year of Sunshine

The angel was at the top of a statue in the middle of a small square. He had climbed up and buttoned his coat around the cold angel.

I have known Lucca for 30 years and its mentality has changed so much. On my very first trip there that fateful summer of 1961, Marco was taking me to Viareggio so I was dressed for the beach in what was known in those days as a 'St Tropez', which is tight pants, low-waisted, and a little top revealing a bare midriff. The locals were scandalised and, recognising Marco, rushed to tell my mother-in-law that it was outrageous that I had walked down the streets like that, upsetting their husbands, and that I was to cover up in future. On another occasion, I remember walking down the crowded main street in pants. We had just driven down from Geneva across the mountains and I still had my pants and boots on. I couldn't understand why everybody was calling attention to me, stopping and staring. I asked my mother-in-law.

'Oh, no woman wears pants and boots in the city. They've never seen it before,' she had replied.

And now they show soft porno clips on public TV in the evenings.

'*Ma* ...' (Oh well), as they say in Italy.

Next day, Florence and Pisa.

What can one say about Florence that hasn't been said before? Ponte Vecchio with its teeming tourists never ceases to amaze me. I have visited Florence dozens of times during various springs and summers and I lived there the autumn and winter that Francesca was born, but whatever the season people congregate around Ponte Vecchio, the Uffizi

A Temporary Truce is Declared

Galleries, and Piazza della Signoria, in their droves. Fiesole, in the hills of Florence where most of the villas are because it is cooler in summer, is sublime. (The heat collects in the valley and is stifling; especially at midday and at night when it feels as though there is not a breath of air.) Cypress trees and olive groves surround stately villas, and it is almost *troppo bello* (too beautiful). In midsummer, the exquisite coolness and the birds singing and that feeling of total peace, is almost holy after the heat and thronging tourists of downtown Florence.

I know of two monasteries there. One is very big, half way up, and has been turned into a five-star hotel called Villa San Michele. It still has some of Michelangelo's statues and a fresco, and the Villa Medici is nearby. The other is much smaller and is at the very top of the hills. It is still being used as a monastery and church. The peace there is absolute.

Pisa is, of course, unique with its leaning tower, which really does look as though it will fall one day. And there were the tourists being photographed with their hands positioned as though they were stopping the fall.

After five days, we drove back to Golfe Juan. I couldn't believe it, but I was almost happy to see the boat again. I believe I had almost missed it, but there was still a bittersweet edge to our relationship.

The next day, Sunday, was another sparkling, glorious day. Anna and Fabio in their boat, and we in ours, motored out to the islands to swim and sunbathe. This really was the most idyllic way of life, as long as everything went smoothly.

During the following week, we took Francesca and Luke to see Port Grimaud, where I had planned to return to explore. There were a lot more tourists than when we were there in May, but it did not detract from its beauty. The architect had caught perfectly the atmosphere of a little fishing village and had expanded on it, glamorised it, and the result was spectacular.

The canals, where the white sailboats and motor yachts were moored, the quaint shops and colourful restaurants, the houses with their small flower-filled gardens, and the little humped-back bridges across the canals, all added up to an enchanting fairy-tale picture. We resolved to return with the boat and stay for a couple of weeks later in the season.

St Tropez was only another half an hour further on, according to the map, but we hadn't bargained on the number of tourists on the road. We were stuck in a queue for almost two hours which was unbearable in that heat but, when we finally arrived, we were rewarded by a small but endearingly cluttered port. It was colourful with a disarray of boats—big ones, small ones, with no apparent order—and the pavements crowded with artists showing their paintings and tourists looking on.

The little town behind the port is, perhaps, prettier than the port itself. It has narrow, winding cobblestone streets, zigzagging up and down, and the air is perfumed with garlic and marinara sauce.

We returned to the boat that night tired and hot, but happy.

The next day we planned to go sailing but I was saved by a *Mistral* warning, so we enjoyed Golfe Juan on bike and foot.

We drove to Italy the following day, and enjoyed a wonderful Italian meal in a seafront restaurant in Alassio. First, Camparis all round, then *spaghetti agli scogli* (spaghetti with a

A Temporary Truce is Declared

mussel and garlic sauce), followed by *fritto misto di mare* (fried seafood), and for dessert, *frutti di bosco* (fruits of the forest including wild strawberries, raspberries, blackberries and red currants sprinkled with lemon and sugar). All accompanied by a local wine and sparkling water.

We explored *il budello*, a long narrow winding street parallel to the seafront, but one block back from it, which is crammed with shops where you can find the best bargains (*il budello* actually means intestines). The streets are paved with cobblestones and closed to cars and it is always crowded with shoppers, both local and tourists. The outdoor cafés and *gelaterie* are kept busy. The apartments above the shops are ancient, with narrow winding stone stairs—moving new furniture in must be a nightmare. Here the smell of cooking wafts in the air and conjures up all sorts of delightful culinary creations.

Back in Golfe Juan, the next day was 14 July. It was Francesca and Luke's last day and also Bastille Day. There were to be great celebrations all over France, but the Riviera was going to excel itself. Juan-les-Pins and Cannes were putting on big fireworks displays and Golfe Juan was having an open-air concert at its *théâtre de mer*.

We spent the day swimming, motoring out to the island, and doing all the beautiful things that one does on the Riviera. It was another white-hot, sparkling day, and in between activities we lay around talking over Francesca's holiday, very sad they were leaving. They had had a truly wonderful holiday. Their enthusiasm for the boat had really helped me, and I think I almost progressed to 'liking' the boat now. Certainly I loved the lifestyle, and while we were

The Year of Sunshine

moored in port or motoring (lucky for me there was never any wind) I tolerated being on the water.

As the evening drew in, the crowds started gathering at the restaurants and bars along the promenade, and they did a roaring trade in ice-creams, coffees, pizzas and crêpes. It was a happy, holiday-makers' crowd, festive for the occasion.

Francesca wanted to go over to Cannes in the boat to watch the fireworks display from the water, but Fabio and Anna had a previous engagement, and I wasn't brave enough for us to find our way over there and back, plus moor in the dark, all on our own.

We had dinner and were sitting out on deck drinking our coffee and finishing our wine. It was a beautiful evening, still warm from the hot day, with a slight evening breeze that caressed, and the sky was full of stars. There was a happy buzz from the crowd on the promenade. People on their boats were drinking, eating, enjoying the balmy evening, and there was a wonderful *joie de vivre* atmosphere.

Suddenly, music filled the air. It was the most incredibly beautiful music I had ever heard. It was the 'Space Opera Concert' by Didier Marouani at the *théâtre de mer*.

It filled the port, it filled the sky and it was spectacular in its delivery. It was unlike any music I had heard—exciting without being overpowering, magical without being weird—and it was accompanied by coloured laser beams and images shot into the sky. It was sensational.

We all sat, as if in a trance, unwilling to speak in case it broke the spell. Francesca started to cry.

A Temporary Truce is Declared

'How can I ever describe this when I go back?' she whispered emotionally. 'I can say the words, but I will never be able to explain this feeling.'

It was one of those perfect moments, one of overwhelming beauty.

Sitting there on a yacht in the French Riviera, listening to that incredible music would be hard to describe. She was right—it would be almost impossible, but we would have known it, and that's the main thing.

It finished around midnight with a fireworks display, but we were not tired. Our spirits had been lifted by the music and, along with a couple of thousand others, we went for a long walk along the promenade, past the port, along the beach, never wanting this night to end.

But end it had to, and we eventually fell into bed while the last of the stragglers finished their coffees and drinks and let the restaurant and bar owners close up around four.

Marco and I made love passionately that night. More passionately than we had for a long time, in fact, since he had announced his decision.

We lay in bed, arms wrapped around each other, breathing in the sweetness of profound intimacy and passion shared. I was happier than I had been for a long time and I'm sure he was too.

He hugged me closer to him and kissed my forehead.

'Angel, I love you so much. I would give anything if it could always be like this again,' he said.

'I know,' I sighed in agreement.

I would have to number it among the most beautiful nights of my life.

The Year of Sunshine

We took the children to the airport later that day. They were deeply tanned and relaxed and looked wonderful in their Italian outfits, new leather jackets thrown around their shoulders. They didn't want to go, we didn't want them to go. We waved our last tearful waves and returned to our lonely boat.

Emptiness overtook us and the boat, and we spent the day finding all sorts of jobs to fill our time and occupy our minds. I was glad that last evening had been such a success and it seemed appropriate that it had happened on their last night. We had laughed a lot at our clumsiness and lack of knowledge, my fears and Marco's fearlessness, and it helped me put it all into perspective. Their presence had helped us to start unwinding.

Francesca's insistence on being shown all the places that we knew and loved and that were associated with such enormous happiness had been very therapeutic for us—it was like a lifetime revisited. You cannot relive your youth, but you can and should remember your youthful happiness. It is strangely satisfying and by doing this you sow the seed of new happiness. Marco had been right—not that he had put it quite like that, but the essence was there. He had recognised the need to plant new seeds of happiness and his happiest memories were of this whole area, so what was more logical than to return there.

Showing them to our children had reminded us how precious those memories really were, how they'd influenced our lives and had allowed us to create new ones with them.

The next day, to cheer ourselves up, we drove to Nice, Villefranche and Beaulieu. Looking down on the bay of

A Temporary Truce is Declared

Villefranche from the upper road on the side of the mountain, soothed our emotions. It is a truly great sight, offering a brilliant panorama of colour.

This enormous bay of aquamarine was sparkling in the sunshine, the coastline and surrounding hills dotted with exquisite pink villas and beautiful gardens. The dark conical shape of the ever-present cypresses and the red and pink bougainvillea broke up the various greens of a myriad of different trees and plants. The tiny, old port, characteristically quaint, added its colours of blue and white to the overall picture. The occasional sailboat bobbed daintily in the bay, and on that day a huge white luxury liner majestically waited, and all was being kissed by shimmering sunbeams.

'Don't forget we've got to leave Golfe Juan next week,' Marco reminded me.

Was it really a month since we had set foot on board the boat for the first time? It had felt like a crash course on living. Now we had to start finding our own moorings, something I didn't look forward to after hearing how difficult it was. Moving on every three or four days didn't appeal. It took me that long to get used to new surroundings.

'Where do you want to go?' he ventured.

'Anything close,' I quickly replied, dreading the thought of moving away from my beloved Golfe Juan. I had made myself at home there, and didn't want to be uprooted.

'How about Antibes? That's close,' he suggested.

I shrugged my shoulders in agreement.

'Well, we'd better get some sailing practice in if we're going to start moving,' he said.

The Year of Sunshine

Oh-oh, this I didn't want to hear.

My heart felt as if it had suddenly shrunk to the size and consistency of a small stone and had wedged itself somewhere in my stomach.

'Do we have to?' I felt like a small child who had been told to eat her vegetables, not wanting to, but knowing she had to.

Marco nodded. 'Tomorrow.'

'On our own?'

'Yes, on our own!'

I sighed a sigh of the condemned.

Talk about the agony and the ecstasy with this trip. There was always a helping of terror sandwiched nicely between the bliss.

I slept fitfully that night, praying for a *Mistral* so that we wouldn't have to go out.

The new day dawned golden and hot.

The dog in the boat across the pontoon had also obviously slept fitfully too since he barked almost incessantly from five onwards at anything that moved. This didn't improve my disposition. I was irritated and unco-operative, but I could see I wasn't going to get out of it, which made me worse.

We got out of port without too much incident, with me dashing from side to side pushing us off other boats if we got too close, and went a little way out into open sea.

'We'll practise reefing today,' said Marco.

I couldn't see how we could practise something without knowing how to do it first.

'We'll find out,' said Marco. 'Let's get the sail up.'

There was a little wind that day. Perhaps I had lost favour with the gods.

A Temporary Truce is Declared

We got the mainsail up and unfurled our self-furling jib, and we were sailing.

'OK, shorten the sail,' commanded Marco.

'How?' I wanted to know.

'I don't know, find out,' he said. 'I'll let the sail down a bit, you see if you can work out which rope to pull to secure it.'

Well, I pulled and I struggled. I had seen Fabio put a hook into a hole in the sail near the mast. I tried that, but the sail fell to the floor at the other end of the boom in a great uncontrollable heap.

'That's not right,' Marco shouted over the wind. 'You must pull one of those different coloured ropes and it will tighten up the sail.'

After fighting with the sail and the ropes for over half an hour I was getting near screaming point. The sun beat down relentlessly, and I was hot to the point of boiling. I could feel the sweat on my scalp running in rivulets down my face and neck, and I couldn't keep my glasses on, they kept slipping down my nose. The wind was picking up and I was hanging on to the boom for dear life as it danced me backwards and forwards over the roof of the saloon.

'This is too dangerous for me,' I yelled, the wind carrying my voice away, expecting him to see that I was going to end up in the water.

I'll say this for Marco, he was really concerned for me—he threw me a lifejacket!

I put it on with one hand while clinging desperately to the boom with the other, but it only made me hotter and clumsier.

The Year of Sunshine

'I don't want to do this,' I shouted.

'Stay there. We've got to learn how.' The wind brought his words to me loud and clear.

There were times like this I could easily have sunk the boat, and walked away from it without a backward glance. I was terrified of the thing, apart from the fact that I am physically no match for a 44-foot sailboat. In addition, I had no idea what I was doing, which was bad enough, but neither did Marco, and that made it worse.

He could see he wasn't going to get any more out of me today, so he decided to get the sail down and motor back to port. We agreed to ask Fabio on the next weekend how to reef a sail.

We also had to move moorings within the port that week, since they only had our place next to Fabio free up to 18 July and we still had another week to go.

They had given us a new mooring several pontoons over amongst the motor yachts, facing the opposite direction to the one we had before. This time my cabin, the back one to port, faced the afternoon sun and it became like an oven. I hated it. I hadn't thought about it before, but some moorings are definitely better than others. In our first mooring, my cabin got warm from early morning on as soon as the sun rose, but cooled down nicely by the afternoon. In this mooring, it was going to heat up like an oven in the afternoon, be hot to go to bed with and be cold in the morning when you needed it to warm up in the early morning dew.

Being amongst the motor yachts was noisy and smelly. The smell was of diesel fumes as they warmed up their engines

A Temporary Truce is Declared

before taking off in the morning, usually about seven. And the noise was from the cooling water outlet pipes of the air conditioners. Since motor yachts sit higher in the water than the sailboats, you can get the running water noise all day and all night right at your pillow level if you're unlucky, like I was with this mooring. It drove me crazy.

I was in a very bad mood that day and the next, but soon discovered that breakfast and lunch on deck at this mooring were much nicer because it was cooler, so it had its compensations.

Marco, of course, was totally oblivious to all this.

'Who cares which way the boat is facing,' he had retorted when I mentioned it, 'it doesn't make the slightest difference to me.'

And it didn't. He adored his boat; he was a free spirit again. He played with it all day, raced his bike around the port finding bits and pieces to improve it, ate well, and slept like a log at night. He was like a child with a new toy. What more could a little boy want?

He realised though, that we needed to get away from the boat sometimes, so we drove down to Italy at these times. Sometimes we went to San Remo and had lunch or dinner at a favourite trattoria. It was here that I discovered *minestrone alla Genovese* (minestrone with pesto sauce) and *polpi con patate* (boiled baby octopus mixed with boiled yellow potatoes and dressed with an olive oil, lemon and parsley dressing). We also did a lot of food shopping there since we found that we could buy our Pernod, Campari and wine much cheaper, and find great pesto sauce and Italian specialties, and some marvellous fruits and vegetables that weren't always available in France.

The Year of Sunshine

Roberto and Gina (Fabio's sailing instructor friends) were to spend the last weekend in Golfe Juan on our boat, since Fabio's boat was already full. We were taking both boats out to Cap d'Antibes. I was always happy when they were with us, they did the sailing and I could enjoy the trip.

It was the last weekend that we were going to see these wonderful people for five or six weeks since both Roberto and Fabio were going to be skippering boats going to Greece for August.

We had a great weekend in wonderful and fun company. We laughed a lot as Gina recounted a story about another trip they had when they got a seagull drunk on bread soaked in whisky, the poor bird was weaving about the deck in a drunken stupor until it passed out cold. They nursed it back to health of course, but after that the bird wouldn't leave them until they threatened to book it into Alcoholics Anonymous, and it flew away.

I knew I would miss our new friends, and wondered if we would ever see them again.

We exchanged addresses and phone numbers. Who could tell?

Chapter 8

Antibes

The day I had been dreading perhaps more than anything in this whole trip had finally arrived. We had to change ports on our own. I spent the day before psyching myself up for it. It was not a long trip, but getting out of the port, sailing there, getting into the other port, using the radio to find our mooring and actually mooring, all on our own had become an awesome event to me.

Marco was excited rather than apprehensive.

We got up early but we took quite some time to prepare the boat. Taking down the awning was complicated. We took off the gangplank, folded it, carted it downstairs and laid it on the bed in one of the aft cabins. We had bought a teak one because it was more beautiful, but it weighed a ton and was cumbersome to manage. By the time we secured the microwave, TV, radio, coffee pot and flowers, it was getting on for close to ten and was getting hot.

Marco started the motor, and untied the boat from the

mooring rings. I untied the front anchor rope and stayed and watched until the rope disappeared, as was the normal procedure, then waited to give him the signal to go. The rope took ages to disappear and just floated there in the water. It had done this when we had gone out at the weekend with Roberto and Gina, but it hadn't caused any problems, so I wasn't concerned, it just meant I had to wait a little longer. Anyway, Marco was getting a bit impatient since we were no longer tied up and had the motor idling, so he called out and asked if there was the problem.

'The rope doesn't seem to want to go down,' I called back.
He came up and peered into the water with me.
'Strange.' he said. 'Oh well, let's hope for the best, it's almost gone now.'

We started motoring out of the berth and I quickly went from side to side keeping the boat away from the neighbours. You could only start nosing into the canal when you had cleared your neighbours' boats and anchor chains, which brought you a fair way across because of the narrowness of the strip of water, and having achieved this part, you then had to smartly turn into the canal, missing the anchor chains and bows of the boats opposite. Roberto and Fabio had remarked how narrow these moorings were, but we'd always managed, so didn't give it another thought.

We cleared our neighbours' boats and chains, and Marco started to point our bow in the direction of the middle of the canal, when the engine cut out. It had never done this before. He restarted it. It cut out again. I could see the chain from another boat straining under our hull and could presume only that we were hooked on something.

Antibes

What we didn't know was that we had caught our propeller on the floating anchor rope.

'Shit!' Came the angry outburst. 'Now what do we do?'

We were stuck diagonally across the narrow canal, blocking entrance and exit, and I prayed that nobody would want to come or go while we were stuck there.

As luck would have it, at our bow was a young playboy with his motor yacht. He had been rushing to and fro most of the time while we had been preparing our boat to leave, but had disappeared. He reappeared now, his arms laden with baguettes and drinks, and was obviously on his way out for a lunch party. He was, understandably, quite irritated by what he saw, and had a French tantrum. I was terribly embarrassed by this whole thing, and all I could think of was to say *'je m'excuse, je m'excuse'*.

By now Marco was yelling to me to radio the *Capitainerie* for help. I knew how to use the radio but was a little nervous of it. Although I speak adequate French I wasn't sure I could explain myself properly and I didn't want to be asked a stream of questions that I couldn't understand or answer. I didn't know how to say, 'we're stuck in the middle of the canal, and my propeller seems to be caught on something'. I can order haute couture in French, but sailboat vocabulary was still a bit of a mystery to me.

The Frenchman had rushed off to get some help from the *Capitainerie* also, so by the time he got back with three men, I had managed to ask for help (they understand English at Golfe Juan fortunately) and three more men turned up. Here we were with an audience of seven, which I didn't need. All I wanted to do was go below and hide till it was all over. No such luck.

The Year of Sunshine

I had to help the Frenchman's three men keep the two boats apart by pulling ropes and pushing boathooks while the playboy made his precarious exit, with an insolent shrug thrown over his shoulder at us.

In the meantime, Marco was having a conversation with our three from the *Capitainerie*. They were telling him they had to get a diver from Antibes.

'Oh my God, how much is that going to cost me?' asked Marco, annoyed.

'Around 250 to 400 francs, more or less,' they replied.

'Is there no other way?' asked Marco.

'Not unless you want to go down,' they said.

Marco had no desire to go down into the polluted port water. In France and Italy, the toilets flush straight into the port water (other countries require boats to have holding tanks, we found out later) and everybody avoided the port water like the plague.

Marco, furious with himself, sighed in resignation, and we sat down to wait for the diver. It was getting very hot now, so we took it in turns to sit, one on deck and one at the radio, in case they called us.

About an hour later, a rubber dinghy turned up with three men on board, one in a diver's suit. We proceeded to try and explain in French what had happened.

'That's all right, I understand English—I'm Irish,' the diver replied in broad Irish brogue.

'That helps,' said Marco. 'How much?'

'500 francs,' said the Irishman.

'What! The *Capitainerie* told me 250 francs,' exploded Marco, outraged.

Antibes

'Well, they got their prices wrong,' said the Irishman. 'It's 500 francs.'

'You're just getting rich at my expense,' responded Marco, irritated.

'Look at it this way,' answered the Irishman, 'you're sitting up there on your yacht, and I'm sitting down here on this rubber dinghy. Who's the rich one?'

I had to suppress a laugh.

'Hmmm,' grunted Marco, not impressed. 'Get on with it then.'

They freed us quite quickly, and I was relieved to learn that it was quite a common occurrence on the Riviera, although I still wished it hadn't happened to us on our first solo trip.

The amusing Irishman had put me at my ease, though, and we were ready for our second attempt to leave. It was a hot, still day, and nothing would have induced the sails even to flutter had we put them up, so I was delighted that we were able to motor to Antibes without incident.

We had checked out our position the day before from land when we had reserved the spot, so we more or less knew where to go. Although, I must say, it is quite different seeing a place from the quay, and seeing it from the water. But we found our way there and, luckily, it was at the end of the pier so there was plenty of room to manoeuvre.

As we drew in, two or three young men appeared, ready to receive our mooring ropes. I threw them, and they moored us. Easy. It was wonderful when this happened—it took the pressure off me to jump across. Not being an athletic person I wasn't sure I was judging the distance correctly, so had

The Year of Sunshine

visions of jumping short and ending up inelegantly sprawled over the pontoon, or directly in that dirty water.

More people appeared from nowhere and helped us put the heavy gangplank across. It was a nice feeling that everyone was ready to help everyone else.

Antibes is quite different to Golfe Juan. It is huge by comparison, and very old. The ancient fortress on the skyline is lit up at night, making a very romantic setting. The old city is walled and sits perched up on the hill beyond the old wall arches. The port promenade is landscaped with shrubbery and bright Riviera flowers and the whole effect is delightfully Mediterranean. It is a great favourite with the tourists, especially the English-speaking ones. In fact, they have their own little community with a shopping gallery of only English shops in it, one of which was a video shop with English-language videos which we ended up using quite a bit. (Francesca had brought us over a duty-free VCR, which we hooked up to our TV.)

The town itself is ancient and hilly with narrow winding roads leading up and down and round about. It has an old marketplace and an artists' area, and has an enchantment all its own. We loved exploring all the back streets on our bikes and always came across with something new.

Marco was loving our new lifestyle and I was warming to it, and we hadn't realised how much it was changing us until Australian friends, who were staying in Paris, wanted to visit us for a couple of days. We gladly agreed and went to the airport to pick them up. My girlfriend, all elegant from Paris, stared open-mouthed at us, and then started laughing.

Antibes

'I've never seen you like this, you're both so different,' she exclaimed.

I hadn't noticed. The transition had been gradual and I hadn't realised it, but Marco, previously pale and slim from overworking, was now deeply tanned, had gained eight kilos and sported a short grey beard and had his dark hair sleeked back in a ponytail, as was the fashion on the Riviera. And I, usually made-up and groomed for business, was also dark-tanned, wore no make-up, my long hair was in a ponytail, and totally unlike me, I was wearing a denim shirt and short shorts.

Being moored at a place for a period of time, you get to meet the regulars from up and down the quays, and we learned that we had some interesting neighbours. Kings and princes and artistes numbered amongst our neighbours compared to the rich at Golfe Juan. We were in good company quite obviously.

By now, it was around the end of July, and the weather was hot, and the humidity sickening. After a light lunch on deck, I would be completely devoid of energy and would sleep stretched out under the sunshade until about four then the port, and I, would start coming to life again.

After lunch, Marco would generally go and play bridge in Cannes, which left me free most of the afternoon to do anything I pleased on my own, which I loved. I would write letters, do some shopping, or just chat to neighbours up and down the pier.

It was during one of my afternoon siestas that I heard a sudden commotion. I sleepily stirred and lifted my head to see what all the noise was about and could see a large sailboat, about the size of ours, being pulled in by several small port tugs. There was the skipper and a woman, and two young fellows on board, looking very harassed and concerned, hot and agitated, and, as the boat came into the mooring, the ropes weren't ready, the boathook couldn't be found, and there was generally a lot of fuss getting the boat tied up.

Luckily for them, the guys who helped us moor appeared again and helped them.

There was an Italian flag on the boat, so I asked them in Italian what was the problem. The owner said it was a new boat, one year and one month old to be exact, and they had been going to sail up the coast from Italy for the long weekend. It had been a hot, airless day, and they had to motor. After about six hours' motoring, the motor had burnt out. They had been close enough to Antibes to radio for help, and the tugs had gone out to help them.

The thing that got them was that the guarantee on the motor had expired one month earlier.

It was a beautiful new boat and they were really upset at the prospects. They tried to get a motor mechanic that afternoon, but there is little sense of urgency on the Riviera, especially in that heat, so they had to wait around for the next day, or the next, for someone to turn up. When he finally arrived, he said that some part of the cooling system had been put in wrong at the factory. This sent the owner scurrying to phone the factory where he bought it. They denied all responsibility, and more days were lost waiting for their representative to come out to see the motor. By this time, the owner, a doctor, had to get back to his patients, and had to leave the two young men on board to take care of everything.

The representative of the company came out and because the guarantee had expired, would not replace it free, but wanted to charge the owner the price of a new motor, which was around 40,000 francs.

But there was also a problem with replacing the old motor because it was situated in the main saloon under one of the lounges, and was too big to take out of the companionway door, so they wanted to cut the top of the boat off.

The owner was absolutely outraged and couldn't believe what they wanted to do to his beautiful new boat, and wouldn't let them do it, of course, but his alternative was almost as bad. They had to dismantle the entire engine on the floor of the main saloon, bit by bit, and take it off the boat, bit by bit. But the oil and dirt from this would have been horrendous. The boat had been beautifully decorated inside with light colours and cream carpets, and the teak work was all in the palest yellow. I really felt sorry for them having to pay another 40,000 francs on top of what he had already paid for the boat last year. But these things happen with boats.

I kept my fingers crossed for ours.

Two days after this poor boat limped into the port, we had our first experience with the *Mistral*. The *Mistral* is a violent wind, which originates in the Rhône Valley and blows towards the warm waters of Marseilles, but the massive barrier of the Alps restricts its path into the Mediterranean. It is known as a mountain gap wind, and for those living in Provence is one of life's hardships, and can be very destructive.

The Year of Sunshine

There is always a warning when the *Mistral* is expected, because it moves into an area with devastating speed. Whenever we heard the warnings we didn't even think about going out, because we'd heard stories of boats getting into trouble and radios not being able to get through to the *Capitainerie* for help because everybody is calling. In short, chaos reigns, and I didn't want to be part of it.

There's a lot of myth and rumour surrounding this wind. They say it can go for one day, three days, five days or even nine days—always odd numbers. I don't know how true any of this is, but its forecast prompts concern on the Riviera because it is so destructive. It can fan forest fires to tremendous proportions in the hot, dry weather. We were aware of several during the summer, around the Marseilles, Aix-en-Provence area, and along the *autoroute* on our way to Nice after we had bought the boat. The area is prone to fires and the blazes can be frightening and dangerous. Often drivers leave their cars because the visibility is reduced to zero due to the smoke.

Because of the ever-present danger of the *Mistral*, you make it a habit to listen to the weather forecast on your boat radio several times a day, every day. It is given continuously in two or three languages—French, English and, sometimes, Italian. It's quite hard to understand because the speech is so rapid and the accents so strong that sometimes you have to listen to it three or four times before you get the message.

This day, we had heard the warning for the *Mistral*, but since we weren't going out we paid little attention. We were in port, having an after-lunch nap. Marco was not going to

Antibes

bridge that day, so I slept with him in the cabin. The *Mistral* came up at great speed and brought a storm with it.

At first, we just heard the wind sighing through the masts and halyards, so we knew a wind was coming up, but we were not prepared for what hit us. Within minutes, we could hear the halyards whipping against the masts, the lashing gaining momentum. The wind started howling and the boat started rocking violently. Thunder crashed around us and the lightning lit up the now black sky in great jagged white streaks. The rain was torrential, and the wind ripped and tore at the sunshade. Everything was happening at once. It was as though all the rages of hell were let loose. We rushed up on deck to make sure our mooring was secure and we were practically blown off the deck. The force of the wind was unbelievable and we hung on to anything we could grab hold of. The bow anchor had broken loose, and we were being blown sideways, up and onto the doctor's boat. The strength of the wind was absolutely incredible and we desperately, but uselessly, tried to push ourselves off. The wind and rain were furiously battling us, stinging our faces, blinding us, and our great heavy boat was being pushed with all its might up against the other one which was already straining at its anchor.

The doctor and boys rushed out to help, but to no avail, cursing their further misfortune. One of the boys grabbed a rope and jumped over to the boat on the other side of us. How he did it, I don't know. All the boats were straining at their ropes and chains, dipping up and down and the boy threw the rope around the mast, tied it, and threw the other end over to us. We hooked it round our front anchor cleat and pulled with all our might. Little by little by little, we started gaining against the wind. The doctor and the other boy came and added their weight to the pulling and we started coming off their boat slowly. The four of us pulled on that rope as though our lives depended on it, fighting the wind and rain, struggling to keep upright, slipping and tugging until we got a bit of leeway. We tied more ropes to the other boat until the wind abated, maybe a half an hour later, with as much speed as it had come up, leaving a trail of destruction in its path and floating debris in the now-calm water of the port.

We had felt like a cockleshell being dashed to pieces in the port waters. I didn't ever want to find out how we would have fared had we been in the open ocean. I could understand now why people rushed back to port whenever a *Mistral* was forecast.

The poor doctor must have thought his boat was destined for total destruction on that trip, between the motor and then us ending up on top of him. Luckily no damage was done, but after that, we always made sure we had two ropes on the front anchor as a precaution.

Rain is not pleasant on a boat. You have to close all the portholes, and it gets stuffy and hot, but if you open anything the rain pours in.

This was our first experience with rain on the boat and, luckily, it didn't last very long, a couple of hours maybe, but those couple of hours were enough to soak anything we hadn't carefully closed the portholes against.

One day, not long after the *Mistral*, when we went to Italy, I left my cabin porthole open because it was so hot, but

Antibes

there had been a storm during the day and when we got back my bed was completely soaked, as though somebody had thrown a bucket of water over it. We were always very careful, after that, to close the portholes and deck hatches tightly whenever we left the boat.

Antibes was a very busy port. It was less private than Golfe Juan, and there was always a great deal of action up and down the quays. In fact, cars could be parked directly in front of our mooring, which meant you could keep an eye on your car, but at the same time, people were always coming and going, so it was very noisy. You could say it has a lot of port atmosphere, with shouting, and talking, boat bikes and cars, workmen and crews, and of course, it was nearly August when almost all of France takes a holiday and seems to come to the Riviera.

We were very lucky that we had been able to get five days' mooring by saying that Carlo from Golfe Juan said to Jean-Jacques of Antibes that perhaps he could help us. We were learning the system. On the surface, it appeared to be the same old story, it's not what you know but rather, who you know. In the end, this turned out not to be true since the Riviera that year had had a million less visitors and, in addition, had also opened two or three new ports to lessen the congestion. The combination of the two meant there were always one or two berths available if they liked your face. But we really only found this out later, and for the time being were under the impression that the former was true, and probably had been up to this year. In fact, we were able to extend our stay to nine days by using this formula (or so we believed).

The Year of Sunshine

There was always something going on in Antibes. There were always new faces, new boats coming and going especially around us since we were in a non-permanent spot. We'd get to know our neighbours, and the next day they would be gone, with new ones to take their place. We were hearing stories of their travels, their lives, and their fortunes, lost and found and usually lost again. (The owners of the fortunes that were not lost usually kept to themselves and retained permanent crew on board. They usually had the motor yachts, so we got to hear about the crew members' lives.)

They were such a mixture of nationalities: German, Dutch, Belgian, English, Swedish, American, Swiss, just to name a few, plus lots and lots of Italians, mainly from Milan and Genoa. The Italians mainly owned the sailboats, the other nationalities the motor yachts, and there was always comparison between the two types of boats. I went on board a few motor yachts, and they were very glamorous. I think I wouldn't have minded a motor yacht, but Marco insisted they were dangerous because they were higher and didn't hold the waves as well, and of course they were madly expensive to run considering the price of petrol in Europe. They are also extremely powerful with their two engines, and, one day, an elderly man, when trying to moor, jammed the reverse gear, and almost ended up on the quay after writing off his tender and ramming his neighbour's boat.

A similar thing happened in Golfe Juan when a youth who was getting his father's powerboat out, misjudged, and literally ended up on the pontoon. It was awful, but comical, seeing that motorboat sitting there on the pontoon as if it had been parked there purposely.

Antibes

Such are the joys of life in a marina.

I felt I was finally making progress with life as a yachtie, but my relationship with Marco was another thing entirely—good one day, bad the next. One thing I had no control over was the heat, which apparently collects in Antibes because of the Alpes Maritimes, and which had been almost unbearable that year. I'm not exaggerating to say the temperature reached 45 degrees sometimes, I know it was hitting 40 in Paris on occasion.

During August, things were happening in Australia, the recession was starting to feature in newspaper headlines, a couple of big entrepreneurs had gone under, and later, the Property Trust collapse in Victoria filled the business sections. We were following a lot of this news in the *Financial Times* and *Time*. We would get the paper and settle down on deck with breakfast or lunch, whichever was the case, split the paper up between us and read it over our coffee, speculating on the outcome of these events.

And so our stay in Antibes drew to a close. It had been fascinating and different, but we had to move on.

After visiting Port Grimaud again with Francesca, we had decided we would make our way up to that part of the coast slowly. We decided to stay at St-Raphaël, about half the way to Port Grimaud. We called the port the day before and they had a berth for us for a week. We'd been in luck again.

During our months searching for a boat, we had visited and liked St-Raphaël, suggesting it as a possible place to stay. It was pretty and clean, had an old part near the *Capitainerie*, which was near a huge parking lot, and a new part, which was opposite the marina.

The Year of Sunshine

We had an uneventful, peaceful trip, motoring in the 42 degree heat. I was glad I was on the boat, at least there was the slight movement of air as the boat motored at six knots. We had a nice easy mooring, although I couldn't understand the number they had given me over the radio because it kept cutting out—Marco insisted it was me not working it properly—and they had to come and yell the number out to us, which was a bit embarrassing since I didn't catch it that way either.

It was a disappointing week and a bit flat after the hectic pace of Antibes.

It was pretty and practical, with a whole shopping centre built on the marina, but it was not an international set that gathered there, like our previous places, and we had a mooring in the old part. (For some reason, we had expected to go into the new part which was pretty and faced the marina shops, restaurants and bars.) I sat on deck, eating breakfast, facing a huge parking lot that had obviously been a cleared building site—not very inspiring. I was horrified a couple of days later when a huge caravan of lorries and mobile homes arrived and set up sideshows of sharks and barracudas, and we had loud music and thousands of people milling around to see the show, for several days.

We had a motor yacht moored beside us with its air-conditioning pipe running day and night. However, the owners of the boat, a French lady and her husband, both over sixty, and he wearing an obvious toupee too dark for him, were very nice, and I spent occasions talking to the lady who sat and read on deck every day.

The flatness of pace allowed me the opportunity to do a lot of thinking, and while Marco went in search of a bridge club, I appraised my situation. I thought about my life right now and where it was heading. I thought about the ports we had stayed at, and all the things we had experienced so far, our exit from Golfe Juan and the anchor rope, the Mistral and the doctor's yacht, Francesca and Natasha back home, my life in Sydney, my future on the boat, and my relationship with Marco which was the main reason for coming. While I could admit that a lot of it had been beautiful and some of it fun, I could see that we were at a stalemate.

We were not moving forward as I had hoped, and it was probably because I did not feel comfortable with the thought of spending the rest of my life as a yachtie, moving from port to port, following the sun to Spain during the winters, and generally being a nomad. Cleaning the decks, and washing and cooking in a cramped space with little convenience, I found needlessly difficult, and quite boring.

It was slightly better in a good tourist port, since there was always something else to do to distract me from mundane chores. However, while speaking to our Italian friends it seemed that not all ports were good or interesting. Some were dull and downright boring, others ugly and inconvenient, but the overriding factor for dedicated yachties was the freedom of spirit which living on a boat allowed. Unfortunately, this wasn't a top priority with me.

I liked a certain order and discipline in my life, I liked to know I was in control of what I was doing and using. I needed to know I could pick up a phone when I wanted, not wait in a queue at a public booth. I wanted to flush the water in the toilet, not pump it. I wanted to use a washing machine again, not hand-wash things every night and have them hanging from anything that protruded or wait at the launderette (when you could find one) to wash sheets and towels.

On the other hand, it was a top priority with Marco. He found the freedom of being a yachtie stimulating enough to override the inconvenience. (Let's face it, he did not wait in phone queues or hand-wash anything—I did.) He loved the open-air and the nomadic lifestyle. He loved spontaneity, hated predictability. For the first ten years of our lives together, we had lived and worked in five different countries. This had provided him with enough freedom and unpredictability to satisfy his soul, and afforded me a certain degree of mental stimulation—learning a new language and working in it—and comfortable living in rented houses or apartments, and I was happy too.

After being settled for the last 20 years, he wanted this freedom and unpredictability back. He loved Sydney, but he needed to be free to travel again. As far as I was concerned, Sydney suited me fine and provided me with everything I needed as a working mother.

It was obvious at this point, that as much as we loved each other and wanted to put our relationship right, we had separate agendas.

Perhaps I should leave. I could offer to spend summers with him, but I knew he would never consider that. For him it was always all or nothing. I would have to be always there or never there, there would be no half-and-half. He would construct a new life, I knew him well enough to know that. He would make new attachments and leave the old ones behind. Would I be able to cope with that, I questioned myself? Well, it would be my choice, painful as it would be. I could see no future for myself on the boat, and if that was what he wanted to do with his life, I could no longer be part of it.

Maybe we had come to the end of a long, long chapter. It seemed such a shame to end it this way, when we had spent so much of our lives together. Thirty-odd years of living side-by-side and making a marriage work was already an achievement on its own when you consider the disparity in personalities. But perhaps there comes a time in some people's lives when they both want something different. How do you deal with that? Perhaps a parting of the ways is the only answer.

Maybe it had been foolish to come, to even consider that I could put things right, since it all really depended on how I took to the boat, and I had strong preconceived notions about that. On the other hand, I may have loved life as a yachtie, then Marco would have been happy and we would both have moved forward together. But that wasn't happening.

I knew it would break my heart to leave him. It was a huge life-changing decision not to be taken lightly.

Did I fully see the implications? Apart from the obvious heartbreak and painful disruptions to family life, the apartment would have to be sold, a smaller one bought, eventually Francesca would marry and move out and I would be alone. Perhaps if I returned to Sydney at the end of summer Marco would miss me enough to … to what? He had pretty much made his decision about his life, so why should I expect him to change it because of me?

The Year of Sunshine

Did I really want to do this? As I saw it, I had no choice. Life on an ocean wave was not for me. Oh, I had made great strides over the last months. I had thrown off a lot of the trappings of my previous life. I had overcome a lot of challenges, and gained enormous knowledge about another life, but did I want to immerse myself in it forever? I could take it in small doses—summers I could do, but lifetime, no. It was as the Italians say, *più forte di me* (stronger than me). Why do something that would break my heart? The question went over and over. Because it's not possible for me to do what he wants and we would both be unhappy all the time, was the answer that came up.

I wondered how he would take it. There would, no doubt, be long discussions and arguments. 'Well, let's talk about it,' he would say when I suggested something he didn't really want. The talk could turn to long heated discussions in true Italian fashion, until I had convinced him he was wrong or he had convinced me I was wrong. Perhaps it would clear the air.

I would have to choose the right moment, of course, and I decided to sit on the decision for a while just to see how it felt. I wanted to be able to change my mind.

But at the moment I could see no other choice but to leave Marco at the end of the summer and try it on my own back in Sydney.

Chapter 9

Port Grimaud

I had, as a precaution, since it was August and the Riviera was getting very full, called Port Grimaud two days before we left, and the young lady at the *Capitainerie* promised to save a berth for me up there for a week. This was unusual, but due to the circumstances described earlier, they did it, and again we counted ourselves lucky.

However, we must have managed to get one of the last remaining moorings because during our stay we saw several people who turned up hoping to stay the night or a couple of days who were told to leave because it was fully booked.

We left our mooring at St-Raphaël overlooking the empty building site easily, we were glad to see the back of it.

From this part of the coast up to Marseilles, the wind starts. For geographical reasons, there is always wind, to some degree. In fact, that day, although it must have been 35 degrees, there was a nice breeze, and Marco said that we should sail for a while.

The Year of Sunshine

I was not very happy, of course, but since the wind was behind us, blowing in the direction we wanted to go—Port Grimaud—I didn't think it too much of a problem. I hated the thought of having the sail up just in case I had to reef it, or some other complicated thing that Marco would think up and that we didn't know how to do. Anyway, we sailed for an hour.

I didn't feel this was a great achievement, since I was apprehensive the entire time, much to Marco's annoyance. As we got closer to Port Grimaud the wind started to change direction a bit, which meant that we had to change the sail slightly if we were to end up where we wanted to go. We did not know about compensating for the tide and, try as we may, we continued going straight ahead instead of turning in towards the coast as we wished. We tried it this way, and that way, but we were being blown off course. We had absolutely no idea what to do to rectify it, since we had done all the things we thought we knew. I was getting more scared and Marco was getting more frustrated, and I was relieved when he finally decided to get the sail down and continue with the motor.

We got the sail down, which was always a laborious job for me because I had to do the physical pulling, while he stood at the helm steering the boat and managing the winch. It was exhausting if the wind was strong because I was battling the wind as well as bringing the great sail down, then trying to tidy it up along the boom without falling down the companionway (which I invariably forgot to close before I went up to do the sail). I was always stressed out when I finished after being bounced back and forth as the wind caught the boom with the great sail draped over it.

Port Grimaud

About half an hour out from port, I asked Marco if I should radio ahead and let them know we were coming and get the number of the mooring, which was the usual procedure.

He nodded.

I went below and got on the radio. 'Port Grimaud, Port Grimaud, Port Grimaud, this is *Sunshine*, over. Port Grimaud, Port Grimaud, Port Grimaud, this is *Sunshine*, over.'

Nothing but crackling. I could hear other messages being transmitted, but cutting in and out and crackling, then silence, then more crackling. For 20 minutes I tried, again and again, unsuccessfully. I was convinced our radio wasn't working. The oppressive heat, below deck, was unbearable, my stress level increasing, and sweat was pouring out of me.

'What the hell's taking so long?' Marco called out impatiently from his position at the helm.

'I can't get the radio to work,' I replied lamely.

'Are you sure you are doing it right?' he yelled.

'Yes I am,' I shouted back. 'It's not working. Come and try it yourself.'

Irritated, he made me take the wheel while he tried. And he got through first try. 'Why are you so useless?' he shouted furiously from down below.

'Why are you such a prick?' I shouted back, cursing under my breath that I didn't want the goddamn boat in the first place, and why was he so unfair.

By now, we were almost at the port entrance. The girl at the *Capitainerie* had told him to radio her when we were there and she would show us where to moor because the canal system was a bit complicated.

The Year of Sunshine

The *Capitainerie* was just inside the entrance to the port. I had never seen such a busy port in my entire boat life. Antibes was busy, but Port Grimaud topped it. Small boats, big boats, motor yachts, sailboats, tenders, even rowboats trying to get in and out. It was a very anxious manoeuvre in. We stopped outside the *Capitainerie*, and I tried to call. The radio would not work again.

'Keep trying,' he ordered.

The radio was as dead as a doornail. It was just crackling and crackling. They weren't replying.

'Port Grimaud, Port Grimaud, Port Grimaud, this is *Sunshine*, over,' I started again, repeating it and repeating it.

Nothing.

Marco was on deck trying to miss the fleet of boats that were trying to exit and enter the port. I was below trying to get through on the radio. We couldn't go anywhere because we didn't know where to go.

I called and called. Finally I started calling, 'Port Grimaud, Port Grimaud, Port Grimaud, please help me. We are outside the *Capitainerie*, please help us.'

I could hear other boats calling too, but do you think I could raise a reply?

By this time, I had no sweat left to pour out of me and my stress level was exhausted.

Marco's stress level, on the other hand, was still mounting. The heat, my imagined incompetence on the radio, and our precarious position were getting to him.

His Italian blood was boiling over, and he was hurling insults at me.

I retaliated by shouting at him to come do it himself if he

thought he was so bloody smart.

He yelled back angrily that he wouldn't be able to trust me to miss all the boats that were trying to get in and out.

I was sorely tempted to push him overboard, but I just abused him some more, not realising my hand was still on the 'speak' button on the radio microphone.

I must admit it was a rather hair-raising situation for a pair of novices like us.

At this point, he was beyond all reasoning and started hollering out to the *Capitainerie*. By this time the entire port should have known we were there. At long last, a young lady jumped into a tender, came over to us, quickly handed us a map, and said, 'This is your number. I'm so busy, I'm afraid you'll have to find your own way there. My radio isn't working properly. I can hear every word you say, but no-one can hear me.' Then she turned round and dashed back. She spoke good English—I'm sure she speaks it quite a bit better now as she would have learned some choice new words from us.

The joy was to continue.

We found our way to our place, and as usual, it was all different.

Every port has a different system for mooring and different electricity plugs. You'd think for the sake of the poor newcomers they would use universal plugs, at least.

However, we found our place and I started looking for the front anchor rope, which is normally attached to the pontoon. You bring it along the side of the boat with the boathook, and secure it to the bow mooring cleat.

No anchor rope.

The Year of Sunshine

We looked and looked, and asked some people but they didn't know.

We thought ours must be missing, but were told by a man watching, intrigued by what was going on, that we must use the buoy in the middle of the canal. We had seen the big red buoys in front of each berth and, while trying to push ourselves off the boats beside us that were moored so closely together, had thought what a stupid place to have this buoy in the middle of where we had to go in.

I ran up the deck to the buoy wondering how I had to use it. I could see no obvious way of mooring ourselves to it. I suppose had I been less hot and a great deal calmer, I would have worked it out quite quickly, but I just stared stupidly at that red buoy.

Marco was involved with tying up to the pontoon and was shouting out to me to get a move on.

Get a move on to do what? I didn't know what I had to do. Nor did he.

Seeing our confusion, a neighbour on another boat called out in French to use the buoy.

How? I picked up the buoy with the boathook hoping the mystery would be revealed to me. Nothing.

What do I do now?

'Use the rope,' they were calling out.

What bloody rope, I thought to myself.

There appeared to be a black rope attached to the buoy. This must be the rope they're meaning. I fished it up with the boathook.

'*Non! Le bout!*'

'What the fuck is a *bout*?' I was talking to myself now. I

didn't know. I shouted down to Marco. He didn't know either. Now confused by the entire operation, he was jumping up and down at the other end of the boat, offering me everything from our cockpit storage but the right thing.

Finally, a guy jumped over from another boat, picked up a mooring rope, slipped it through the buoy and anchored us.

'There, wasn't that easy?' he said to me in French, a sarcastic smile on his face.

'Eat shit and die,' I muttered under my breath, hoping he didn't speak English, the smile of gratitude on my face disguising the murderous thoughts I was feeling.

At this point, I was wishing the water would open up and just suck me in, but no such luck.

We were in for more fun. None of the plugs would work, of course. However, on the positive side there was a TV aerial plug in the utility box. Marco was pleased about this because he had spent numerous hours pursuing a decent TV antenna for the boat, but none were really efficient because of the rocking of the boat.

He rushed over to the supermarket and came back with a bag full of plugs and aerial wire.

'Now sit here and help me wire these plugs,' he said to me, settling himself at our deck table, and he threw me the TV antenna and a set of plugs. We know as much about wiring plugs as we did about sailing when we first set foot on this boat. We had an electrician change the plugs at the other ports, and it had cost us 350 francs a time—daylight robbery, or tourist robbery, is what it should be called—but at least it was hassle-free and done in ten minutes. Now we

The Year of Sunshine

sat and pondered over the array of plugs set out before us, and made several unsuccessful attempts.

The port was full of yachties and day tourists, and quite a little crowd had gathered to watch us. After all, we were providing them with an afternoon's very good, free entertainment. He started asking if anyone in the crowd knew how to do it. I wanted to die.

Nobody offered, they just smiled sheepishly and shook their heads as though it were part of a well-rehearsed act. I just beamed back at them, desperately wishing I knew a good disappearing trick.

It took us about two hours to change four plugs. By this time, it was about five in the afternoon. I felt I had done my 'act' by playing the part of the fool all day long, and I was exhausted and desperately needed to lie down.

I went down to my cabin and threw myself on the bunk in utter dejection, when suddenly my eyes caught my open porthole, and I realised that the big old motor-sailer that was moored so close to us, was higher than us and its hull was almost touching ours because the fenders were so squashed. But what bothered me was that their bilge outlet pipe, was smack, bang in the centre of my open porthole, and all I needed was for them to have a shower, and we would have been able to save water. I was so exhausted and depressed I realised I didn't care any more. Not too much more could happen to me today, and if it did, it would be a drop in the ocean.

The end of summer couldn't come quickly enough for me. With it I could see a light at the end of this long, dark and tortuous tunnel, and it was this thought, and this thought only, that got me through that first horrendous day. Our arrival had done nothing to convince me that my decision was wrong. I was reminded again how out of my control everything was. I must have been crazy to think I could ever contemplate living on a sailboat.

Our stay at Port Grimaud turned out to be almost as eventful as our arrival.

After we had sorted ourselves out, and calmed down with a couple of stiff drinks, we settled down to a fairly quiet evening of TV, which we could see perfectly now because of the new aerial, but, tired out, we both fell asleep early that night. The next day, we set about exploring Port Grimaud. You actually don't set about making new friends, it just happens in a port.

The big old boat that was next to us on the day we arrived, had moved and now there was a glorious turquoise and white motor yacht beside, all done out with white carpets and white lounges, which were the last word in luxury, as far as I was concerned. It was owned by an Italian who manoeuvred it into the narrow mooring beside us, as though he and the boat were one, he did it so skilfully.

He was constantly washing it down, or I should say, the two young crew were constantly hosing it down, with water spraying into our open portholes all the time. He had taken on board, as crew, a young brother and sister. The brother helped run the boat, and the sister did the cooking, washing and ironing, for the owner, his young wife and little daughter.

On the other side of us, we had another delightful Italian family. The parents, Guido and Patrizia, were sailing enthusiasts, and they had their little boy, Vittorio, with them. He

The Year of Sunshine

was about one and had virtually been born on board the boat. Patrizia had taken him on board almost as soon as she had been able to get up from the hospital bed, she loved sailing so much. He was the dearest little boy. They were from Milan also, like every other Italian we had met on this trip so far. We made great friends with them. Apparently they had also had a very eventful arrival, arriving the same day we did.

They had actually booked months ahead for a good, quiet spot, because of the baby, and when they arrived they were told to wait at the entrance until their berth was vacated by somebody else. They had waited there for about two hours. As I said before, the port was chaotic that day but they had been told to wait there so they put down the anchor. When they were finally told to go ahead and move, he got his propeller entangled on a loose anchor rope, and he too had to get a diver to untangle him; he was very annoyed and frustrated.

Anyway, he moored next to us, and as he was at the end of the block, he should have had a nice peaceful berth, since this was where a new canal started leading to a bridge, which denied access to sailboats.

Unfortunately for him and because it was August, a huge tourist sailboat had been allowed to moor along the quay from the bridge and alongside him, almost reaching his bow. It was a monstrous thing, big and wooden, old and touristy, with people clambering on board from the queue, which gathered for every trip out. It went out three or four times a day for a sail round the coast and was a big attraction. Because it was so big, it had trouble manoeuvring and every time it came and went it had a problem missing our neigh-

Port Grimaud

bour's bow, because it had to go around him to go out to sea, or around him to moor. Every time it passed he rushed out to make sure it didn't hit his boat, because he too had a beautiful, brand-new boat, and he was very proud of it.

Understandably he was getting quite upset about this because he had come up to Port Grimaud to relax, and he just couldn't do that.

Every morning we would either walk or take our bikes to get fresh croissants and bread, and have breakfast on deck. The place was thronging with people. Whatever you did on your boat there was an audience of two to three deep watching you. You ended up feeling like performing animals.

We started eating inside, but every time we looked up, there were faces peering down into the boat trying to see inside. They were only curious, of course. I suppose they thought it was a sort of huge boat show, where they could share life on board with you, or at least fantasise about it. It became a little bothersome in the end, but it was too hot to close the companionway door, so we had to live with it.

We had a wonderful time exploring the area. The main square was cobblestoned and full of restaurants with tables outside shaded by the omnipresent coloured umbrellas. There were rotisseries selling any kind of roast you required—suckling-pig, chicken, lamb, beef, veal—sold by the slice. There were prepared-food delis so you could virtually buy every meal out but eat it on your boat for a fraction of the cost and without the hassle of waiting to be served.

There were fireworks displays, and dances in the square and markets that came and went. There was always something going on.

The Year of Sunshine

We explored the surrounding areas on our bikes. We rode up to the next port, Cogolin, which was still being constructed in a similar style as Port Grimaud, and between the two ports, there were huge shopping complexes with everything you could possibly need.

We explored further out still, in the car. We drove up to Grimaud, a delightful little town perched on top of a hill overlooking the port. These ancient little towns were always strategically placed for viewing the enemy, and there were sweeping views of the coastline for miles around.

And so a week went by and a truce was established between us—assisted by the enchanting surroundings, we were so delighted with the place we asked to extend our stay. They said we could stay four more days but would have to change moorings.

Guido, our neighbour, was booked to stay another four days anyway, but he also had to change moorings since the owner of his berth was returning.

I was delighted when another neighbour, having seen our arrival, offered to help us move. Marco was offended, I was relieved, and apart from almost ramming one of the ever-present little tourist boats, full of sightseers, it was an otherwise uneventful move.

Guido's was a bit more troublesome. He had to move later in the day, and as the morning wore on the wind started coming up (there had been warning of a *Mistral*) and try as he may, he couldn't get the boat into the right position, and had to attempt it three or four times. He finally did it, only to discover there was no utility box with electricity and water there, so he had to use a shipping agent's close by.

Port Grimaud

To make matters worse, the wind was picking up strength and more boats were coming in seeking haven from its torment and were being moored two and three deep in some places. They were squeezing them in anywhere they could, it was so crowded—a port is obliged to accept boats in bad weather even if there are no moorings left.

That night the *Mistral* picked up speed, and continued ripping and tearing at anything in its way for three days. It was really nerve-racking living on the boat with the wind howling, and everything flapping and rocking mercilessly.

We avoided going out because it was extremely unpleasant, and the dirt and dust that was being blown everywhere made it impossible to eat outside, and the restaurants were really having their patience tested. Nerves were frazzled and tempers flared (it is a fact that wind raises blood pressure) and stories of damaged boats abounded.

The boat was getting filthy from dirt and dust, dead wasps and leaves, and the water was full of pollution and muck. By the third day, I was dying to get off. It was so confining and the sound of that relentless wind was really winding us up. We were due to leave in two days, and I prayed that the *Mistral* would have blown itself out by then. We were to go back to Golfe Juan until the end of August for a couple of reasons. One, it was the only place where we could find space available, but we were not unhappy about that because I loved Golfe Juan and would happily have moored there permanently. The other reason was that Natasha was coming to join us in early September. We were to pick her up in Rome, so we thought we would take the boat down to Italy, closer to Rome, and Golfe Juan was a good stop-off before continuing down.

The Year of Sunshine

On all our previous moves, we had moved the boat first, and then Marco went back for the car by train or bus or both, and brought it down to the port we were staying at. This time, I thought, why not go down first and leave the car, and then train and bus back. It was also a good idea generally to go to a port the day before arrival, pay a deposit to secure a place and check out the number of the mooring. It was a good excuse to get out as I had missed my usual weekly trip to Italy because Port Grimaud was too far away for a day-trip.

Marco agreed it was a good idea and since it was our last day, we had Guido and Patrizia for lunch, but baby Vittorio slept longer than usual, and we ended up leaving at four-thirty instead of two-thirty as planned. We were lucky we didn't get a speeding ticket as we raced down the A8 and made Golfe Juan just before six, parked the car, put a deposit on the mooring and ran to the train station.

We knew the train went just as far as St-Raphaël, and then turned inland, making it possible to reach Port Grimaud only by coach. The coach ran every 90 minutes, so we hoped we would make the connection in time. We arrived in time to catch the eight o'clock coach, along with quite a crowd of others. It took ages to get everyone on board with their backpacks and bags, and it was annoying to discover that the bus filled according to destinations, starting with the ones closest to St-Raphaël and ending with Grimaud. We had been among the first to arrive, expecting to get a seat together for the long coastal drive up, and instead we had to wait till last, until we complained that this wasn't fair, and they let us take the last double seat.

Port Grimaud

It must have been after eight-thirty when we finally left and dusk was drawing in. We sat back and relaxed, realising we wouldn't be back to the boat until at least ten-thirty or eleven, depending where the coach left us, for although we asked for Port Grimaud, the driver kept saying Grimaud, the town, not the port, as though he knew we hadn't understood.

About 45 minutes into the journey, still on the beach road, but getting away from civilisation, the coach broke down. It was not a good place for it to break down considering that it was almost dark, and there was no other form of public transport other than the next coach in a couple of hours' time. There were a lot of young people on board, some in pairs, some travelling alone, and I felt sorry for the ones on their own, wondering how they were going to manage. I also wondered how we were going to manage.

'We'll have to hitchhike like them,' said Marco. I looked doubtful, seeing the other 38 passengers lined up at the roadside with their thumbs out. At least there was a little light from a couple of bars way back, although there were no street lamps. Cars streamed by with no intention of stopping. They certainly would have been astonished seeing a busload of passengers thumbing lifts.

Surprisingly, one car stopped and took on a load of kids, but we could see how hopeless the situation was and the group started to spread out further along, and further back down the road, to separate ourselves and have more chance.

Now I've seen it all, I thought, shaking my head. I've never hitchhiked in my life and I have to start now? After a little, a shout went up the line that the bus was fixed. The driver and a couple of passengers had fixed it. Everyone was relieved. They didn't like their chances of being picked up either. We all piled back in, exchanging reassured smiles. Our relief didn't last long. Ten minutes further up the road, it broke down again.

If the first place it broke down was bad, this was worse. We were off the coast road and were heading slightly inland. It was pitch black and the chances of being seen as the headlights flashed by were nil.

Shit! I thought. What now.

'Quick,' Marco whispered to me, 'Get off the bus. At least we can be first to hitchhike before the whole bus load tries again.'

In my haste, I tumbled off the bus and fell into a ditch that I couldn't see. I couldn't see my hand in front of my face it was so dark. Marco sees better in the dark than I do, and he guided me quickly down the road to a rounded bend. We were lit up momentarily as each car flashed by. This is not only hopeless, but also hopelessly dangerous, I thought as I stepped back into another ditch to miss a car speeding past.

I thought ruefully about spiders and snakes, and tried to dismiss these nightmares quickly, realising I didn't know if France had dangerous spiders or snakes. Ignorance is bliss, I decided.

This went on for ten minutes or so and I thought, 'If they could see me now, my family and friends would have died laughing at the prospect.'

Oh God, please send us a car soon, I implored silently.

As if on cue, a car pulled up in front of us with a woman driving.

Port Grimaud

Totally convinced my prayer had been answered, I cried, '*Oh, merci, merci,*' while opening the back door and scrambling in, followed by Marco.

'*Vous êtes très aimable, Madame.*'

'*Attendez, attendez, qu'est-ce que vous faites?*' (Wait a minute, wait a minute, what are you doing?) Madame said.

'We are going to Port Grimaud, what are you doing?'

'I'm going to Port Grimaud too, but what are you doing getting into my car?' she was understandably alarmed.

'We need a lift. The bus has broken down. Weren't you stopping for us?'

Her headlights were picking up the stranded passengers now making their way up and down the road.

'No', she said, 'I'm supposed to pick up my son from around here, his car was stolen, and I've lost my way. I was going to ask you for directions.'

My face dropped. I felt so stupid.

'But, of course I will give you a lift', she said smiling.

Oh thank you God, I said silently, smiling gratefully.

It turned out that we had more in common than the drive up to Port Grimaud. Without a further thought for our poor companions left behind, and with a silent vow to pick up all hitchhikers from now on, we sat in comfort discussing the fact that she and her husband also had a Gib'Sea 44 Master, which was a real coincidence since there weren't many around.

With many thankyous and promises to look out for each other, after picking up her son she left us at the entrance of the port.

I was very relieved to be back.

Chapter 10

Decisions, Decisions

Next morning, we got up early, prepared the boat and left for Golfe Juan. The *Mistral* had blown itself out and a beautiful day had been born, with hardly a breeze, the sky a brilliant blue and the sun not ferocious.

The hours of flat-sea motoring without distractions of sails, reefing, compensation for tides, wind, wondering how the new port would be set up, since we already knew Golfe Juan very well, afforded me a perfect opportunity. It was time to tell Marco of my decision.

He stood at the helm and I sat beside him on a cockpit seat. We talked about things in general, our experiences in Port Grimaud, our new Italian friends and their baby, Natasha's impending arrival and Golfe Juan.

'How are you feeling about being on the boat now? Are you getting used to it?' he asked, innocently.

I looked at him, a dark sunburnt, good-looking man, hair pulled back, short grey rugged beard, wearing only swim-

The Year of Sunshine

ming trunks and sunglasses, his hands on the helm. My heart went out to him. Oh God, what am I doing? I love this man, how can I leave him, am I crazy? I hesitated, but I knew I had to do it and this was as good a time as any if there is ever a good time for something like this.

'You know I love you, Marco. I really love you.' I started, 'I came on this trip just for you, you know that, but I was not born to be a sailor and I cannot contemplate being on the boat for the rest of my life. I can't see this working out in the long run, so I have decided to go back to Sydney at the end of the summer and give it a try on my own, as much as it kills me to do it.'

He was visibly stunned. His grip on the wheel tightened, whitening his knuckles, and he stared straight ahead, his face set.

I could feel his pain. I could feel my pain.

I wanted to get up and put my arms around him, and tell him it was all going to be all right. But I didn't. I stared out at sea waiting for the explosion.

It didn't come.

Silence, except for the sounds and sights around us, the motor, the seagulls, the flat sea, the blue sky, the sun shining down. I even felt as though my heart stopped beating.

He said nothing. It was as if he had not heard me. It was as if I had not said it.

I wondered what was going on in his mind.

My momentous decision, the decision I had tortured myself with, tossing it backwards and forwards, suffered over, had been met with silence. There was no verbal reaction, no response.

Decisions, Decisions

We stayed like that until we reached the entrance to the port.

We motored to our spot, tied up, fixed the fenders, put the gangplank on, set up the sunshade, still as though my words had never been spoken.

I was not going to repeat them in the hope of provoking a response, I would have to wait until he was ready, but I felt relieved that I had said them. My decision was now out in the open. I would go home in a month or two and start my new life, however hard it would be without him. I felt better that there was an end in sight and that he knew what was in my mind.

I was happy to be back in Golfe Juan, in a port with which I was familiar and I helped hose the boat down and do the chores willingly. We were put in a temporary mooring next to an old wooden boat that was being repainted and lacquered and the smell from the lacquer was terrible, so I was very pleased when another sailboat turned up and the skipper said that we were in their place.

It was late and he said tomorrow morning would be fine for us to move since they had been given something for the night anyway.

The next morning, the wind that had come up during the night was now fairly strong, but since we were only moving two pontoons over, Marco didn't want to go to the bother of taking down the awning all over again. An American from the other boat came over and offered to help us move. I was delighted again, Marco offended again, but I insisted the man help, and I'm very glad I did.

'You go over and be ready to catch the ropes when we're mooring, then,' said Marco.

The Year of Sunshine

'Don't you want to take this awning down first?' asked the American.

'No,' replied Marco, 'don't worry, it'll be fine.'

'The wind is fairly strong,' said the American, 'it might act as a sail.'

'We're only going two pontoons along, I'm sure it will be all right,' Marco insisted.

They untied and started coming out of the canal. The wind was catching the awning and it was filling out, then flapping empty, and it was with difficulty that they reached the end of the canal before proceeding along and down to our new mooring. The boat was being blown haphazardly along, and by the time they reached the new mooring twenty minutes later, the wind had increased and the awning was now filling out more. The wind had ripped the securing ties out of the eyelets where I had tied them to the guard rails, encouraging the great white sheet to fill out like a parachute.

I could see the poor American getting quite panicky by all this, rushing from side to side, trying to push our boat off the other boats, while Marco tried to manoeuvre through the narrow canal. By now half the port had come out to see this spectacle, and here we were once again with an audience.

Finally, the two men decided they should get the awning down and they fought the wind to release it, and at last managed to moor the boat.

I was glad I had insisted that the American help, although he, I am sure, must have regretted his offer.

We settled into our new mooring nicely, but the toilet in my bathroom had not been pumping properly, and now wouldn't pump at all.

Decisions, Decisions

'I'll get Jean-Michel to come and fix it for me,' I told Marco.

'Find out how to do it yourself,' he said predictably.

I went down to the tiny room and looked. I could see that the toilet bowl unscrewed right off and that several pipes leading to and from could be disconnected, but I wasn't game to do something that could sink the boat. It was a tiny room, barely big enough for a toilet and washbasin, although it was beautifully compact, but it was hot and I didn't fancy it.

'I'll try and find Jean-Michel,' I told Marco.

Jean-Michel came by later that afternoon, took one look and said he didn't have time that day or for the next week.

'Did he know anyone in port who would come and do it for me?' I asked him.

He shook his head.

'But you can do it yourself,' he shrugged, in that French way of his.

'How?' I grimaced.

'Well, you undo the green pipe,' he said, 'unblock it and wash it out. But it might be the valve, so be careful that the water doesn't flood the boat.'

This I needed to hear.

'I'll do it tomorrow,' I resolved grudgingly.

The next day was difficult—it had been hot and tempers had flared frequently. Marco was in a very bad mood and I was unco-operative. Considering this, it was probably a bad decision for me to attempt to fix the toilet.

I undid the little metal belts holding the green pipe on and tried to remove the pipe. I struggled with it for nearly an hour, cursing and swearing and blistering my hand. The smell was

The Year of Sunshine

horrific because as I was loosening it, sewage was seeping out. I was almost sick and had to tie a cloth over my nose and mouth. But, however hard I tried, I couldn't remove the pipe.

Marco was sitting on deck reading the paper, purposely ignoring what was going on below. It was quite obvious to me that the announcement of my decision had hit home finally. He could hear all the swearing and cussing, but was being temperamental and bloody-minded, and paid absolutely no attention to it.

Our neighbour, a well-known Milan architect (although we didn't know it at the time) in an elegant motor yacht, was sitting on deck having a pre-dinner drink. He could hear all the commotion from our boat.

We knew they were Italian because of their flag, and we'd smiled and said our *Buon giornos* and *Come stas* the previous day, but nothing else so far.

'*Cosa c'e?*' (What's the problem?), he said to Marco, nodding in my direction.

Marco told him.

'Let me have a look,' he said.

This lovely man, elegant in a beige safari ready to go out for dinner, came below and found me on my hands and knees, hair screwed up out of the way and covered with an old tea towel, another tea towel tied over mouth and nose, red in the face from anger and sweat, and cursing like a sailor.

'*Torno subito*,' (I'll be right back) said this elegant man.

He came right back with a mask (why didn't I think of that?) and with one swift effort, wrenched off the tube, and whoooosh, there was *caca* everywhere. The stench was overpowering. He ran, almost falling up the stairs in his haste.

Decisions, Decisions

Marco jumped up, and they almost collided at the gangplank, both escaping off the boat from that terrible smell, and I was left with poo and pee up to my ankles.

I thought I was going to pass out, the smell was so revolting.

It would have to be the most disgusting, revolting job in the world. I sloshed buckets of water and disinfectant everywhere and sent it all down the bilge pump, but it took me the best part of an hour to clean up. (Now I knew why Jean-Michel was so unhelpful.)

We had to try the pump again. It still didn't work. Piero, the elegant architect, said this wasn't good news, because it probably meant the toilet pump itself was broken and would have to be pulled apart, and that was a big job.

He didn't have time now, he said, they were going to dinner, but he would help us tomorrow. It would probably mean that Marco would have to go down under the boat and check what was going on. Marco didn't think this was a good idea, since everyone hated the port water. I hoped he didn't think I would go down.

I woke the next morning not knowing how the day would unfold. Would Marco go down into that filthy port water, would he expect me to go down, or would Piero go down? He didn't seem to mind it so much, saying he did it all the time.

He came over after breakfast and I installed myself in the little bathroom with all the tools. I would let the men work it out between them who was going down. Piero came down wearing a costume and holding snorkel and goggles.

'I'm going down now,' he said. 'Be ready in case I need anything.'

The Year of Sunshine

Obviously Marco had won the toss.

I grabbed the pump pack of liquid disinfectant soap and put it handy so that we could wash him off with the hose on the pontoon immediately he came back up.

He disappeared into the murky water.

Yuk, I thought.

He reappeared almost immediately.

'No big deal,' he exclaimed, 'give me a little sharp knife. It's just barnacles. They've grown completely over the opening of the outlet pipe.'

I sighed with relief. I didn't feel like dismantling the toilet pump completely, which was our next alternative.

He returned soon, offering me a handful of what looked like sharp little dog's teeth.

'It's the hot summer we've had,' he said. 'The warm water encourages the barnacles. Everyone's going to have a problem this year.'

He climbed back onto the pontoon, and we all helped cover him with disinfectant soap and scrub him down. After that we became firm friends—I felt he knew me intimately.

Every day, he and his young wife would take their power dinghy out and dive for mussels. They would prepare them and bring us a plate complete with lemon quarters and a glass of wine. They were such great friends to have and we had many entertaining dinners on their boat, on our boat, and at restaurants in port.

In the meantime, Guido and Patrizia had arrived in Golfe Juan on their way back down to Italy from Port Grimaud. We had booked them into Golfe Juan when we arrived, so

Decisions, Decisions

that they had a place. They came to find us and Guido had a long face.

'What happened?' I asked.

He explained that they had left Port Grimaud soon after we had, but had stopped in St-Raphaël for a couple of days to pick up some friends. There, a big motorboat had come charging into the canal where they were moored and hit their bow and bent all the metal work, doing about 2,000,000 lire of damage. The guy wasn't insured and didn't have a licence, so they were really upset. Then their friends had used too much paper in the toilet (there are no secrets on boats) and blocked the outlet tube, and Guido had had to unblock it, which I now knew was literally a shit job.

Guido and Piero joined us on our boat and we talked about the end of the season, and what they would be doing with their boats over winter. They both moored permanently at Lavagna, past Portofino, and said they would only use their boats on weekends, when the weather permitted. They were both back at work anyway and winter was approaching.

All too soon it was time for Guido to leave, and we exchanged addresses and promised to call in and see them on our way down to Rome.

The weekend came and who should come walking up our pontoon, bags slung over his shoulder, but Fabio. He had returned from his month skippering a boat around Greece, but was now back to move his boat down to Sardinia where he was going to winter it.

We were overjoyed to see each other again, and he threw his bags onto his boat and joined us as we sat down to dinner. We spent many hours recounting our adventures to

The Year of Sunshine

him and he was laughing so much he could hardly speak.

He could barely manage, '*Ma, siete matti, tutti e due!*' (You're crazy—both of you.)

The next night, Piero's wife made us all *risotto alla marinara* with the mussels they had fished that day. We sat on deck on their boat, Fabio, Piero, Lucia, Marco and I.

It was nearly the end of August, and it was considerably cooler in the evenings now. The stars stood out brightly against the dark sky. We sat there with our wonderful new friends, all of us tanned dark brown, with sweaters thrown around our shoulders against the cool air. We drank wine and told stories of the hot and eventful summer, and I wondered how much happier a person could get. I had conquered the summer, the boat and the heat, and I was going back to Sydney soon. Marco had his arms tightly around me, so I still had him too for the moment.

The weekend was over too quickly, and it was now time for Fabio and Piero to leave.

We said our goodbyes, and felt very alone.

Piero, we knew, was stopping in San Remo, on the way back for a day, before continuing to Lavagna, so we thought we'd give him a surprise. We jumped in the car and drove down to the port at San Remo. We found his boat and called out to him from the quay. He couldn't believe his eyes and we all had a good laugh, and went to dinner at a favourite trattoria of ours in the small town, postponing the inevitable parting once again.

But dinner came and went, and we had to get back up to Golfe Juan, so we said our goodbyes again, and once more felt very alone.

Chapter 11

Breakthrough

The last day of August arrived and with it, the end of the season.

We actually thought the season went through to the end of September, but at most it probably dragged through to the middle of September, and I say 'dragged through' because it really did drag. We woke up on the first day of September and it was as if, during the night, a switch had turned off all the magic.

People had been leaving over the last few days and the ports were suddenly empty and quiet. The days were not so hot and the nights were considerably cooler. There was a great emptiness everywhere—the vibrant atmosphere was gone and there was no longer an air of expectation, or an anticipation of fun. The feeling was heavy and sad, like a lovers' parting when the holiday romance was over.

The sky was frequently grey now, reflecting in the sea, making it grey and sad. There was no more brilliant azure.

The Year of Sunshine

Gone was the sparkling turquoise water. The tables with their colourful tablecloths and umbrellas had been packed away. There was an absence of the happy, laughing holiday-makers.

Evident now were the locals, relieved to get back their town, reoccupying their spots at their favourite bars and resuming their walks. The shopkeepers could stop smiling for the tourists, now they were complaining they were tired. They probably were; it had been a long, hot, busy season despite the talk of the million less tourists.

Whole parades of bars and restaurants along the beach-fronts closed, boarded up for the coming winter, adding to the feeling of desolation.

It seemed as though overnight they had barred their doors and windows, locked the shutters and left without saying goodbye. We felt, unreasonably, abandoned.

Uppermost in Marco's mind was what he was going to do next. We could stay in Golfe Juan until the end of September because the owner of our mooring wasn't due back till then, but after that we were on our own.

There were few of us left in port now, living on board. Weekdays were the worst with just two or three familiar faces at best. Weekends livened up a bit with the die-hards taking advantage of the few remaining sunny days, for the last trips of the season.

We discussed what we should do next with the boat. He seemed to include me in his plans. I wasn't quite sure how this was going to work out, but I went along with it waiting for some indication. Neither of us brought up my decision to go back at the end of summer again. But I was adamant—I was going.

Breakthrough

He was toying with the idea of closing the boat up and putting it somewhere for winter and returning next summer. He wouldn't want to do the same thing again next year, he said, always assuming that we could. He would want to go further afield—to the Balearic Islands, Sardinia or Greece.

I certainly did not feel we were proficient enough for such an undertaking on our own, although I would consider going with another experienced sailor. My dread of the sea was diminishing, but it had not disappeared. At least I now knew what I was letting myself in for, and wouldn't go in blind and fearful as I had this summer.

Finding a place to put the boat for winter seemed to be a problem though. We had been asking everyone everywhere if they had anything available during the winter months.

No, they said, everything is booked out, and if there was something available, in the new ports, it was outrageously expensive. Since we weren't sure that we were going to be able to spend the entire summer away from Australia the next year, it seemed like an atrocious waste of money. It was also a worry inasmuch as Australia is so far from Europe we would be unable do anything in an emergency such as storm damage or vandalism. But even so the boat would need checking and airing on a regular basis, and although one can leave these problems with guardians, they are costly and there is no guarantee as to how conscientious the guardian will be.

He looked at the prospects of selling, but that also had its problems.

He chatted about it with several agents. They didn't like our chances of selling since the recession had put a freeze on anything to be sold like houses, apartments, cars and certainly boats, as the future was so uncertain.

We lay on our big double bed, propped up by pillows, discussing all of these points. I reflected on the eventful summer, realising that I would never have another one like it.

My eyes rested on the beautiful teak panelling, lovingly polished, sunbeams from a soft blue autumn sky playing on it through the skylight. I looked at the bookcase, full of the books we hadn't had time to read, and the chess set Marco hadn't had time to touch.

I smiled, as I looked at the beautiful pictures of Port Grimaud that I had given to Marco for his birthday—one of sunset on the sailboats, all glowing pink and port wine red; and the other two showing the fairytale colourful canals and the fishermen's houses in vivid detail. The boat rocked us gently, and I thought again how perfectly perfect this lifestyle was when it all went smoothly.

My thoughts wandered over what I would do with my life if I didn't have a boat.

'I think we must at least try and sell and then reconsider the situation in a couple of years,' Marco said finally.

Surprised, I sat up and rested my hand on his arm. 'But Marco, why are you giving up something you love so much?'

'I'm not,' he replied easily, 'I'm not giving you up. I'm selling the boat. I've got my life back and I've got you back, that's what I wanted. *Ti amo, amore mio, immensamente.*'

'But I thought ...' I began.

He took me in his arms.

'I know what you thought. You didn't really expect me to let you go back to Sydney on your own, did you?' he smiled.

Breakthrough

'But ...' I began again.

'No buts. I love you, I couldn't live without you. You came with me and I love you for that. You tried even though you hated it, and I love you for that. I can always buy another boat, I can't buy another you. I am retired now; I am free to do what I want. Go anywhere, do anything. We are free to do what we want. We have a fantastic future ahead of us.'

Tears slid down my cheeks.

I was overjoyed and terribly sad at the same time. Overjoyed because I didn't have to leave him and return to Sydney on my own, this time my dream was coming true. And I was sad because this summer on the Riviera had been such a unique experience for me. I had come so far in six short months, and yet that six months had been a lifetime. I had learned so much, I had a whole new perspective on life. I had met so many people from different walks of life and discovered so many new and exciting things; I didn't want to let go.

'What's the matter?' Marco was surprised. 'I thought you hated the boat!'

'I did!' I cried, 'but now I love her.' And as I said it I realised for the first time that I was no longer reluctant.

Sunshine had taken me from terror and tears, through to laughter and joy. She had made me face my fears and dispel them. She had forced me to look at my values. I had been seduced by power and glamour, I had equated my sense of self to the success of my boutique, and without it I had lost it. I had found it again through a long and painful inner struggle, but I had found it with the help of *Sunshine*. It had needed a profound shock to shake me up and she had provided that in many different ways. She had also shown me there were other perspectives, other lives, many alternatives and many choices. We can choose to be happy, or not. Life, with its many opportunities, is there for us to take or leave as we wish.

Francesca had been right, I did need to do this.

Marco and I had been so close to losing each other. *Sunshine* had been an intricate and essential part of an incredible journey back to each other.

I kissed him as though my life depended on it, because it did in a way and he kissed me back. My heart was so full of love for him; I knew everything was going to be all right between us from now on.

The next afternoon, with a heavy heart, I prepared the list of details and the inventory for distribution to the boat agents. I fussed around in the boat and took a whole roll of photos, plumping up the colourful cushions Francesca had proudly bought me in Alassio, moving the coral roses to each room and strategically placing them to enhance the shot. It didn't really need enhancing; the boat was beautiful any way you looked at it.

In two days, the Cannes Boat Show would commence. We wanted to go and hand around the boat details to all the agents, and hopefully hurry along the sale. We were told it was a good opportunity because half the Riviera would be there.

We arrived early. It was a beautiful sunny autumn day, and we enjoyed being there. The boats were all decked out in their gleaming white best, the teak decks still newly pale

Breakthrough

yellow, each agent proudly displaying his manufacturer's latest designs. We stopped at every cruising boat, giving the racing boats a miss.

The year's designs were shown in the Deck Saloon versions which featured big panoramic windows. They looked wonderful, but I wondered how hot they would be with that furious sun beating down in August.

We greeted a lot of the agents who we had come to know over the summer.

'Still buying?' some of them asked that hadn't seen us since May.

'No. Selling,' we answered.

They were amused.

We met up with one of the Jeanneau agents we knew from Golfe Juan. 'Come and see our new designs,' he invited.

There was no gangplank, and I jumped across easily without thinking, realising when I had done it, that I wouldn't have been able to do that at the beginning of the season.

We slipped our shoes off, and went below deck. It was love at first sight.

The entire side of the main saloon was given over to a white designer galley, and the interior decor was coral, white and pale teak. There was a round teak table, and coral upholstery on the divan surrounding it. The chart table, with electrical panel, was spacious and well designed. There was a large double fore cabin, and two large aft cabins, each with a washbasin and room to move about and dress in, and two wonderful large, white bathrooms with showers. And what's more, it had an in-mast mainsail, and an electric anchor, all as standard items.

The Year of Sunshine

Marco, behind me, slipped his arms around my waist, and whispered in my ear, 'Is this the one you want to buy when we come back in two years?'

'Oh yes!' I agreed enthusiastically. I couldn't believe my ears. Had I said that?

Chapter 12

Success

We had four days before meeting Natasha, our older daughter, who was due to arrive in Rome on 10 September. She had been in Zimbabwe and Zambia for three weeks. She hadn't been able to get away earlier because of business commitments, but nevertheless after Francesca's enthusiastic account of her holiday, she was looking forward to some late Riviera magic.

We started our journey to Rome by car so that the agents could see the boat in Golfe Juan while we were away. We decided to take it slowly, staying overnight at our favourite hotel in Monte Magno in the hills of Tuscany, where the smell of wood-fires lingered in the air and the morning was crisp and earthy. Our breakfast cappuccino and apple pastry, eaten standing at the bar, seemed like the best breakfast in the world.

We stayed off the highway and took the coastal road down to Rome, stopping frequently to admire the scenery.

The Year of Sunshine

Autumn was coming and as we looked up into the hills, we noticed that great splashes of yellows, oranges and reds had appeared as the leaves on the trees were changing colour with the season. It came to me that this was the first time over the last 30 years of travelling and changing not only countries, but also hemispheres, that I had seen all four European seasons in the same year. The winter snow in the majestic, splendid mountains of the French and Swiss Alps, the bursting blossoms of spring in the lower *Alpes Maritimes* and Italian Riviera, the fierce and fiery sun of summer on the French Riviera, and now the soft, tender days of autumn, as the sun lost its intensity and the leaves changed colour in Tuscany and Lazio of central Italy. I felt very privileged.

We entered hustling, bustling, chaotic Rome, from a ring road, trying to take in the unfamiliar signs and names as quickly as we could, but the speed of the traffic made it difficult to absorb and we missed our exit and went around twice. We were making for Frascati, which Marco remembered from his youth as a cool spot in the hills surrounding Rome. We finally got on the Frascati road by the Via Appia, and wound our way through several little towns before we saw the Frascati sign. We had asked several people if they could recommend a reasonably priced hotel in this vicinity, but they all said most were booked out with conferences.

We arrived in Frascati, which is cradled precariously on the side of a hill, its ancient piazza on probably the only piece of flat ground in the area. Steep, higgledy-piggledy, cobbled roads led down and around and away from it, and we were advised if we were going to look for a hotel, we should park our car in the parking lot set back from the town because no cars were allowed to park in the town itself. There was no way Marco was going to leave his beloved Jaguar in the unattended parking lot, especially with the luggage in it. After all, we were in Rome.

There was one street which wound its way through the town, which was allowed to take cars, so Marco took it, but it was so narrow and steep in parts that he was loathe ever to do it again.

'This isn't going to be much good,' he said. 'We'd better try a bit further out.'

After more driving and asking, we were pointed in the direction of a gracious old hotel set in spectacular grounds full of tall pine trees and flower gardens.

They had one room left. It was a modest room on the third floor; a little basic perhaps, with two single beds and one bedside table, but at least it had an ensuite bathroom and wooden shutters on the windows. Unfortunately, it had the usual assortment of squashed mosquitoes and spiders higher up on the walls, but apart from that it was clean, pretty and quiet—the latter being quite an achievement for Rome.

The pines were what made it glorious, though, and when we opened the shutters we were practically amongst the treetops.

We had a lovely peaceful night and took our time getting up, showering and having breakfast. It must have been close to eleven o'clock when we were finally ready to leave and sightsee a little, so that we would know some good places to take Natasha and not lose a lot of time.

We went to leave our key at reception, and they were preparing our bill.

The Year of Sunshine

'We'd like to stay three or four more days, please,' I said, 'and we need another single for our daughter.'

'*Signora*, we are fully booked from tonight. We have a convention for seven days. I'm sorry,' the receptionist said.

We loaded the luggage in the car, and I make no exaggeration when I say that we drove around for seven hours trying to find a double and a single or a triple for three nights. We stopped at every hotel we came to who in turn told us to try here or there, but with no luck. We were getting so desperate we even drove into a monastic retreat, which looked as though it rented rooms, but the priest kindly told us that only people on retreat could stay. He kindly telephoned around for us, but with no luck.

Earlier on, perhaps just after lunch, somebody had recommended a new hotel high, high up in the hills. We drove there, and it must have taken us a good hour.

'There must be something closer,' said Marco, 'it's going to take two hours out of our day just to drive to the outskirts of Rome, not accounting for peak hour traffic.' So we continued looking.

Every hotel was booked. I was getting tired and depressed. Tomorrow we had to pick up Natasha from the airport, and we had no hotel to take her to, and nowhere to sleep tonight, unless we slept in the car. It was seven o'clock and getting dark.

'Come on,' I said, 'I don't care how far out it is, I'm not looking any further. We take that hotel at the top.'

He reluctantly agreed.

When we finally got there, we saw what we hadn't noticed before—it was a four-star hotel.

Success

'Christ,' said Marco, 'this is going to cost us an arm and a leg!'

'Too bad,' I said. 'Let's go.'

I went inside and was met by the most charming manager at the reception. I explained our plight to him.

'*Non c'è problema, Signora*. We have an introductory offer because the hotel is only just open and we are empty.'

He showed me up to the two most beautiful rooms I had seen on this trip. Elegantly and luxuriously furnished with terracotta tiled terraces and views overlooking Rome, they were perfect.

I gleefully returned to Marco.

'And the manager says there is a direct road down to Rome that only takes half an hour,' I told him.

Gratefully we moved in.

It was a beautiful hotel, strangely incongruous, new and modern amidst the ancient houses, at the end of a long and winding country road that went up and up and up. It was called *Rocca Priora*.

We had dinner in the beautiful pink and grey dining room. We were the only guests, so you can imagine the top service we got.

The next day we picked up Natasha. She was tired, happy, sunburnt and had a backpack full of dirty clothes that she hadn't been able to wash. They were so dirty I was too embarrassed to give them to the hotel to wash, so we did them in a laundrette.

She clicked away with her camera as we showed her Rome. Dirty, noisy and confusing, but still wonderful. We visited Santa Maria Maggiore, the largest Roman church, built in the early 400s but with an 18th century facade. She was disappointed that the gold was dull and dirty, since I had told her about a trip to Rome 30 years ago, when I had visited the church, and my recollection of that shining, yellow gold everywhere had stayed with me many years. We visited the Venezia Palace, which in turn was the Papal Palace for the Venetian Pope Paul II in the mid-15th century, then in 1806 it became the seat of the French administration by order of Napoleon, and later in 1929–44 was the seat of the Fascist government of Mussolini. She was so looking forward to the Trevi Fountain, but it was all under scaffolding.

We passed Piazza Colonna, which is a small square with a large and interestingly designed column in the middle. When we stopped a Roman and asked him what it was supposed to represent, he shrugged and said it represented a square with a column in the middle. We found out later that it was erected by Marcus Aurelius to celebrate his victories in Armenia, Persia and Germany. The reliefs show a vivid account of Roman life, and the column is considered to be the very centre of the city.

We explored the ruins of the Colosseum, which was completed in 80 AD, and had held 50,000 spectators to watch gladiator fights. Natasha loved this area the most. We walked to the Roman Forum, behind the Colosseum.

We visited the Pantheon, which was begun in 27 BC as a temple to the seven planetary gods, and later converted to a church. We crossed over the river and went to St Peter's and the Vatican, which appeared so big to me all those years ago, but so much smaller on this trip. We saw Michelangelo's Pietà, and walked and walked and walked to see the ceiling of the Sistine Chapel, which had mesmerised me thirty years ago. We went to Via Veneto and visited the Church of the Cappuccini built in 1624. The Capuchins are buried inside in five underground chapels arranged as a cemetery, containing a macabre decoration of the skulls and bones of 4,000 monks, and we also saw the catacombs. We did all this, and more, in two days.

We enjoyed eating in Rome. And in Frascati, where we ate at the local trattorias. We had the specialty of the area—*porchetta* (succulent, roast pork straight from the pig, spit-roasted) from stalls in the town square. It was served between two slabs of bread cut from huge loaves cooked in wood-fire ovens and accompanied by a handful of olives from great big terracotta urns. Wonderful, delicious, scrumptious food.

We took Natasha to Lucca, Florence, Pisa and Carrara, as we had Francesca.

She had wanted to see the school in Florence that she had attended when we lived in Fiesole, when she was six. It was also up in the hills, in Bellosguardo, but the opposite side to Fiesole. We had trouble finding it until somebody told us that the 15th century villa had been turned into yet another five-star hotel.

She couldn't wait to get to the Riviera, where she was expecting to have a great time, after hearing Francesca's glowing account.

On the way to Rome, we had stopped at every port, and had dropped off the information I had prepared for the boat agents. They all suggested it might be difficult to sell the boat in Italy because it involved importing it and paying duty, which would increase the price considerably. There was an additional tax on top of that, which would bump the price up even further. But they all took the details and promised to do their best.

So, on the way back, we stopped at every port again to see if there had been any interest at all. A few said they had had some enquiries, but generally the Italians wait for the Genoa Boat Show in October before buying.

We took the opportunity to drop by to see Guido and Piero, who were both moored at Lavagna. They were delighted to see us, and we all talked excitedly about our adventures of summer, and the fact that we were all losing our tans and how they hated being back at work.

They made suggestions regarding putting the boat up for winter, saying they would ask a friend or a friend of a friend, or an agent they knew, if they could help us. We might have to call on their resources if we failed to sell the boat. They tried to encourage us to keep the boat so that we could all meet up next summer and spend time together again.

But Marco had made the decision to sell after much deliberation and soul searching, so sell we must. Or at least try.

The first thing we did when we arrived back at Golfe Juan was to hurry over to the *Capitainerie* to see if there had been any messages. There had been none.

The town was quiet now. It was an ordinary, sweet little French town, transformed from the glowing, exciting chaotic madhouse of summer just three weeks ago.

It was now 15 September and we had two weeks before we had to change ports. Where to go was becoming more of a problem now than it had been at the height of the season.

This was because boats were returning to their permanent moorings after spending the summer in Greece, Spain or elsewhere—their permanent moorings rented temporarily throughout the summer months. Selling the boat didn't look promising either.

We showed Natasha around, and took her out on the boat, but our hearts weren't in it. Hers because the weather and atmosphere were no longer right, and ours because we were preoccupied by other things.

I made my daily trip to the public phone on the quay, calling up different agents each day, trying to hurry them along, but to no avail. I remembered the times I had come down here to call Australia, waiting in a queue in the burning sun, unable to stand the heat, but unwilling to give up my place in the line. Now there was nobody, and a sweater was in order.

The agents in France said nothing was moving, and the ones in Italy said it was too expensive because of the import duty.

We waited ... hoping.

We went to Cannes and Antibes, and although there were more people there, the feeling was gone. We even went up to our delightful Port Grimaud, but even its appeal was no longer there.

We drove up with ease to St Tropez—no more two-hour queues, and had a very mediocre meal at a beachfront cafe.

Natasha couldn't see what all Francesca's enthusiasm had been about. She was scheduled to leave for London and Oslo on business at the beginning of October.

We were getting desperate for a mooring after 1 October.

The Year of Sunshine

I decided to resort to the very kind agent of the powerboat people who sold us the boat in the UK and who had introduced us to Golfe Juan at the beginning of summer. I must have been guided there by divine energy. He said he was putting some powerboats into dry dock on 1 October, and could let us have a place for another month. This gave us a little more breathing space, thank God.

We took Natasha to the airport, a disappointed young lady. When she got home she told Francesca that she was sure the places she had been to were not the places Francesca had described. They were, of course, but it just showed the difference the season can make.

We contacted everyone we knew who could be interested in the boat. I even called the agent in England who sold us the boat in the first place, but he also said nothing was moving because of the recession.

I resumed my silent conversations with my guardian angels who, I felt, had guided me so carefully and safely through this incredible year. I had doubted they would leave me until they were sure I was completely through this metamorphosis, for that was surely what this had been. I would not have been able to get through this alone. They knew it and had been there for me. They supported me when I didn't have the strength; they gave me courage when I had none.

They spoke to me through my tarot cards and runes, and told me we would sell, so I knew it would happen, only when was difficult to answer.

There was one agent from San Remo who showed a definite interest and was sending somebody up the following weekend. We scrubbed and polished the boat, plumped up the cushions, put beautiful flowers on the polished teak table, and sat down and waited.

Nobody turned up.

'People are like that,' the agent said.

Great, I could see myself waiting out this winter, changing moorings every couple of days, or being anchored in a bay with no electricity and water. I was not impressed. The weather was definitely autumnal now. The air was chill in the morning and at night. There was frequent rain and storms. Several days passed, which we filled as best we could by making contingency plans, wishing and willing something to happen.

On our return from a bike ride, we found a note pinned to our gangplank rope from the *Capitainerie*. An Italian agent was bringing a couple up next weekend. We didn't let ourselves get too excited, but we scrubbed and polished the boat again, plumped up the cushions, bought pretty roses, sat down and waited.

This time the couple arrived—friendly and enthusiastic people. They loved the boat, making comments like *bella*, *elegante*, *grandissima*. But they needed a much bigger aft cabin. The friends who always sailed with them were a fat couple, they explained. Marco suggested that they could sleep one in each cabin, since there were two aft cabins. But they winked a wink that spoke a thousand words, and said Italians don't sleep separately.

Oh well, two down, how many to go?

'Somebody will turn up, you'll see,' we told each other.

I was getting anxious to return to Australia. I had been away over eight months. I longed for a proper bedroom and a bathroom where I didn't have to pump the toilet and smell that disgusting sulphur emanation after the first pump of the day.

I kept up a constant dialogue with my invisible angels. I pleaded with them to find someone soon, because I didn't know how much longer we could hold out. Things were getting a bit tense again, I told them. After all the territory we had covered this year it would be a shame to fall back, but they knew what they were doing.

Marco and I spent our time watching videos from the English gallery in Antibes. We went in to see the Gib'Sea agent who had his office there.

'I think I have a buyer,' he said. 'Italians. They know the Gib'Sea Master 44 but they won't pay the price you're asking.'

'But it's in brand-new condition,' we protested. We knew our price was right. We had purposely not overpriced for fear of not selling, and there were a thousand extras.

'Let them see it,' I insisted. 'If they know the boat, and want it for cruising, they'll fall in love with it, and we'll even throw in the TV, VCR and microwave. And, we'll negotiate if we have to.'

'OK. I'll arrange a rendezvous,' he said.

We were torn between being excited that somebody was genuinely interested, and annoyed that we would have to accept a lower price than it was worth, but necessity was starting to take the initiative. We speculated who they might be. If they know the boat, they must want it for cruising, we guessed, since it was the perfect cruising boat, so it must be a couple like us.

Success

So we scrubbed and polished the boat, yet again, plumped up the cushions, bought the lovely coral roses, and sat down to wait.

The appointed time came and went. We started sighing with irritation. Another letdown, we presumed. Marco walked over to the *Capitainerie* to see if the agent was there.

I waited, contemplating the future of a winter on the boat, and not very impressed with the thought.

There were some shouted greetings going on down at the quay at the bottom of our pontoon, five or six men obviously off on a happy errand.

I saw Marco walking up with the agent, Jean-Claude.

'No show, huh?' I said to Marco.

'Oh yes,' he said, 'they're coming.'

I looked for a couple down at the quay, but all I could see was this group of noisy, excited Italians.

'That's them,' he said, nodding in their direction.

My eyes opened wide in astonishment. How wrong can you get, I thought.

Six of them turned up, their ages ranging from 20 to 50. I greeted the smiling, eager group.

They went through the boat enthusiastically asking questions, climbing everywhere.

I know they didn't even notice the plumped up cushions and pretty flowers, they dismissed the TV and VCR, saying they would take down the much searched for TV support, but they eyed the double bed with satisfaction. They were obviously intending to live up to their Latin image.

We could tell they were delighted and pleased.

'Let's take her for a sail,' they said.

The Year of Sunshine

This was the part I had not looked forward to.

I didn't want to display my meagre experience, but put on a brave face, flashed a smile at them, and said, '*Certo!*' (Sure!)

I climbed up to start taking the mainsail hood off while Marco started undoing the gangplank ropes.

'Don't worry, *Signora*,' they said. 'We're sailors, you don't have to do a thing. We want to try it out ourselves.'

I couldn't believe my luck. My invisible angels knew me so well.

The happy group took the boat out and got it up to four knots with the slight breeze that day. They were having a wonderful time. Their enthusiasm was contagious, and I thought again how much nicer it would have been to have had another couple of crew aboard to help me when we had been out. It was fun. But on the other hand we would not have made the progress we did without our own private space and that was obviously what this year was all about.

Marco showed them how to use the Autohelm 7000 and they were fascinated by it and we could tell they loved the boat.

We got back into port and all squashed around the dining table, reminding me of when we had Fabio and friends around the table, eating, drinking and having fun. They told us they wanted it, but would not budge from their offer because of the import duty and other taxes.

I considered our options and I thought if anyone should have this boat it should be this group of fun-loving Italians. *Sunshine* would enjoy showing off her prowess and abilities, and they would get the best out of her.

I nodded to Marco.

Success

'We accept,' he said.

We got down to details, and it was part of the agreement that we should take her down to Genoa, where these new friends came from, to be imported. It was a 15-hour sail and I was not enthusiastic.

'Don't worry,' said Marco, 'it looks like the boys want to come so there won't be any room for you anyway, and it will take the pressure off me.'

I was relieved. I was to go ahead to Genoa and stay in a hotel while Marco came down with the group on the boat. We phoned a contact and asked him to book a room, but everywhere was booked out because of the Genoa Boat Show. But one of the group had a small apartment in Camogli that he would be pleased to let us use while documentation was completed and we exchanged papers. The trip was planned for the following week.

We didn't know Camogli but this turned out to be a bigger godsend that we thought, since we discovered yet another jewel of a place. The little fishing village was quaint and delightful, the apartment was comfortable and had every convenience. In addition, our new friends fussed over our every need, and we ended up spending two and a half magnificent weeks there.

I started packing and preparing to leave but it was very emotional. I was relieved we had sold, but it was like saying goodbye to a dear friend whom I knew I'd never see again.

The days went by collecting packing boxes for the TV and VCR, washing everything that we were going to have to store in England, and making last minute arrangements.

The Year of Sunshine

I took down the pictures of Port Grimaud that Piero had installed for us, and the family photos that I had crammed into a picture frame that had come with the boat. I squashed the much-plumped up cushions into a suitcase with the rest of the pillows and blankets, packed away my beautiful white towels with the blue reef knots embroidered across them, removing any evidence that we had ever been there. The cases were done, the TV and VCR had been boxed and they all sat forlornly on the divans.

The days were showery, but the last night was dry and starlit. I went up on deck realising it would be the last time I would be doing this.

That evening, after dinner, Marco and I walked along the marina, our arms around each other, talking of what we were leaving behind, the discoveries we had made, and of our future together. How the year had started out so badly and had finished so beautifully. We had worked through our differences and had learned to laugh at ourselves again. We had learned to re-evaluate our expectations of each other, and not be so hard upon ourselves. We realised how important *Sunshine* had been to us, without her we might not have made it. And we talked about how much I loved him and how much he loved me.

We had become lost in life's maze almost to the point where we had lost sight of each other, but made a conscious effort to put it right, however hard it was going to be. There was still some residual work and forgiving to be done, but we were now in the right frame of mind.

I went down to fetch the video camera. The wind was sighing through the halyards and I remember hoping it wouldn't rain tomorrow as we were loading the car. I filmed the port by night, catching the sighing wind, and the starlit sky, and our only neighbour—there were just two of us living in port now. The few lights showing on the quay from the last couple of restaurants still open reflected the masts and outlines of the sailboats. The ghostly palm trees lining the promenade created a good backdrop.

I had started the narration of the filming: 'Tonight is our last night on the boat. It's very sad.'

I finished the film, went below and made a last entry in the journal that my daughters had given me at the airport when we left Australia a lifetime ago.

'I am very sad. As much as I hated the idea at the beginning, I loved the boat at the end. The *Sunshine* made me very happy, and I had time to discover a lot of things about myself and about Marco. She gave me time to unwind and perhaps be myself for the first time in many, many years. I learned how to smile and laugh again, and take life as it comes; be gentle again. I think that's what it's all about—being in touch with nature. Seeing spring turn into summer and summer into autumn has meant so much to me. This year will stay with me for the rest of my life.'

I re-read the inscriptions the girls had written on the inside cover, taken from a favourite book of mine that I had at home. Francesca had written:

> 'Come to the edge,' he said,
> She said: 'I am afraid.'
> 'Come to the edge,' he said.
> She came.
> He pushed her ... And she flew.

The Year of Sunshine

Had she known something I didn't?
And Natasha had written:

> *'The secret of making something work in your life is, first of all, the deep desire to make it work. Then the faith and belief that it can work: then to hold that clear definite vision in your consciousness and see it working out step by step, without one thought of doubt or disbelief.'*

I smiled. How true. I was so proud of how supportive of me they had been.

Next morning we were up early. The rain was holding off. We packed the car and I went up for the last time to check and lock the boat. I patted her affectionately as I locked the door, and said a silent, 'Thank you for keeping us safe. And thank you for putting things right between us.'

As I walked down the pontoon, I glanced back for a last look. Goodbye, dear friend. I was glad the sky was overcast; it was easier to leave.

But I was consoled because I knew that this year would stay with me for the rest of my life.

Epilogue

Marco and I never did buy another boat. We talked about it a lot, we even chose a name, but in the end decided to try other ways of spending our summers before thinking about *Sunshine Too*.

After our summer of *Sunshine*, we took the remainder of our boat things to London and put them into storage. Jaguar in London agreed to keep our car under cover for us over winter.

We decided to explore the rest of Europe by car before taking the plunge with another boat. We now spend about six months of the year in Sydney and six months overseas.

The year after we sold the boat, we drove from place to place, country to country missing the permanent intimacy of our sailboat, but loving our adventures and discoveries just the same.

The next year Francesca and Luke got married and spent nine months travelling around Europe in a Kombi van that Marco had bought them as a wedding present. We met them at the post office in Irun, on the border of France and Spain

The Year of Sunshine

and set off to explore Spain and Portugal together, the Jaguar and the Kombi van making an unlikely combination as we turned up together at hotels. Francesca and Luke insisted on sleeping in their van but would join us for breakfast each morning. Back on the road again we would turn off into leafy, shady spots and Francesca would prepare lunch.

Now we visit places that we both want to see, or perhaps Marco will choose one place and I, the next.

We drove to Scotland one year, and saw the wild, windy, cold beauty of the pink and white heather-covered moors, and stayed in B&Bs with breathtakingly beautiful views of the lochs.

Another year I fancied going back to work in England, so that's what I did while Marco walked all over London, discovering places and restaurants.

We returned to Camogli, where we stayed when the sale of *Sunshine* was finalised. We rented an ancient apartment in the port for a month. We'd taken it sight unseen—it was 'Bohemian' with what we considered an 'original' bathroom. Staying in this apartment was a real experience for us, and reminded me that a person's attitude could change a situation from despair to amusement and enjoyment.

Such are the joys of travelling—there is always a funny story to tell and beautiful memories to treasure.

After a trip to the Caribbean, we decided to look into buying a boat again. We make our annual pilgrimage to the Mediterranean and, unlike on our first mission, we casually explore our options. We haven't found it yet, but perhaps one day when the time and the boat is right, we'll buy *Sunshine Too*.

Epilogue

Retirement is actually a lovely time with all sorts of opportunities. I think we can get caught up with a narrow view of success and achievement and lose sight of what is really important—love, family, companionship, and caring about others. These really are the golden years; there is so much fun to be had and so much to see. You are allowed to make mistakes, and the mistakes should make you laugh—you don't have to prove yourself any more, you are already proven.

My relationship with my daughters remained as close as ever despite my fears that separation from them would have damaged it. On the contrary, we all grew to respect each other's independence and the relationship moved to a different level, closer and more satisfying.

My relationship with Marco grew stronger as well. The time on the boat, with its highs and lows, gave us time to sort out our differences. I recognise that the experiences and things that now fill my heart with joy are all somehow reminiscent of the year of *Sunshine*, when we found each other again and renewed our love.

Marco and I love each other more than ever. We don't know what's in the future but whatever it is, we will face it together.

I will never regret the choices I made in that year of *Sunshine*.

About the Author

Monica Geti was born and educated in London, where she worked as a personal assistant to the managing director of a film company in the West End based at Pinewood Studios. At 21 she met her Italian husband and two weeks later they eloped to Geneva, Switzerland. While there Monica worked as a personal assistant to the managing director of a financial consulting company.

Her husband then joined the company as one of the managers and they relocated to South America, moving from the turbulent north to the happy Carioca south. They lived there for a number of years before deciding to experience life on the West Coast of North America, where they stayed until a financial disaster spurred them on to relocate to France. A business opportunity then took them to the hills of Fiesole, overlooking Florence until their spirit of adventure brought them via South Africa to Australia, where Monica embarked on a successful career importing high fashion from France and Italy.

Marco and Monica retired in 1990 when they bought their boat *Sunshine*, and since then have divided their time between Sydney and the Mediterranean.